HAND IN HAND

by Kathy Zebert

Kyle Roberts,
Live life in color!
Kathy Zebert

Editor: Lauren Tweedy
Cover Design: Kathy Zebert, Lauren Tweedy
Author Photo: Melody Hood, Innamorata Photography

Publisher: Words in Color Publishing
wordsincolorpublishing@gmail.com
www.kathyzebert.com

ISBN: 978-0-9967848-2-5

1. Romance 2. Legal Thrillers

Printed in the U.S.A.

For my grandchildren, Michael and Sophia. You inspire me to make you proud, to love with my whole heart, and to live life in color.

Acknowledgments:

Huge thanks to my Fabulous *Hand in Hand* Launch Team and Pam Martin, my amazing proofreader.

Table of Contents

Prologue 1

Chapter 1: Perspective 7

Chapter 2: Partnership Redefined 36

Chapter 3: Emotions in Check... 55

Chapter 4: A Search for Truth... 66

Chapter 5: Music City Roundup 95

Chapter 6: Whose Surprise is This Anyway?.............................. 104

Hand in Hand

Prologue

Emily sat on the red velvet tufted bench in the foyer, watching the ticking second hand of the grandfather clock. It was two minutes until nine, but she had been sitting in the same spot with her purse by her side for nearly half an hour. On any other day, the clock had no importance to her, but it was Tuesday. It was the one day per week she was allowed to leave the estate, and she anxiously awaited the clock to chime nine times.

Looking up to the small security camera Simon had attempted to hide behind a plant on a corner shelf near the ceiling, she knew he was watching. He was always watching. Every single one of the 41 rooms in the estate had a camera, and there were even more on the exterior, scattered all over the 100-acre property. Simon had brought her here almost a year ago, and in that year, Emily had made it sort of a game to scout out each camera's location.

As the clock chimed its ninth dong, the front door made a familiar click to signal it was unlocked, at which point Emily picked up her purse and opened the front door. The car was waiting under the portico, and Bonito was standing, hat in hand, beside the open door. Emily offered him a "good morning" greeting, but as usual, he was silent. Perhaps he spoke no

English. Emily wasn't sure. Regardless, he had never uttered a word to her. His orders came from Simon in Italian, and he followed them strictly.

The car headed up the mile-long road to the front gates of the estate. Emily's eyes glistened as she noticed the beauty of the spring flowers along the way, and when she rolled down the window, she was greeted by the aroma of freshly cut grass. The sights and smells of a beautiful spring morning made her happy. She knew this feeling would only last for a little while, so she closed her eyes in an attempt to keep it in her memory until Tuesday came again.

Today would be a trip to the mall. It was a very quiet trip, but it only took 20 minutes. Emily chose to spend that 20 minutes pushing her brain to try to conjure up some memory of her past. She had little memory of anything prior to Simon bringing her to the estate. Simon had told her that he rescued her from life on the streets. He also said that he was her husband and that she had no family. As hard as she tried, however, only vague memories would reveal themselves. She simply had no alternative to accepting his version of the truth.

Emily's thoughts had consumed the entirety of the 20 minutes to the mall. As the car pulled up to the entrance, she was so anxious for her two hours of freedom to begin that she refused to wait for Bonito to open the door, but he quickly made his way to her and checked the timer on her phone to be sure it was set for exactly two hours. Taking larger strides than normal, she entered the mall.

Where would she go first? Ah, the tea store. Emily loved smelling and then tasting all of the unique teas they had to offer. It was a great way to explore different parts of the world with her senses. Her imagination was the only thing she could control. Simon would never be able to take that from her.

The tea store was just around the corner from the entrance, and as she neared the store, she smelled something wonderfully familiar. They were brewing a pot of sample tea new to the store. Emily recognized the aroma, but she wasn't sure why. It was very distinct; spicy, yet sweet, similar to root beer. It was a sassafras tea.

As she took a sip, a sudden memory tried to make its way to the surface, but then drifted out of her consciousness just as suddenly. "Ugh! Why can't I remember?" Emily mumbled in frustration. She loved the tea and decided to purchase some. Perhaps if she drank enough of it, the memories would come out of the cobwebs and into her grasp.

The next stop was the department store. Simon had only given her fifty dollars to spend, and he always needed to see every receipt. If she exceeded that amount, it would be deducted from her allowance the following week. Emily carefully placed the receipt for the tea purchase in her wallet and walked towards the department store at the opposite end of the mall.

She passed the food court, which usually seemed to make her hungry. It was too early to eat lunch, though, and she'd already had a bagel for breakfast before she left, so she tried to walk a little faster to avoid the urge to waste money on a cookie splurge. But as she got to the end of the food vendors and nearly out into the open walkway, her senses were greeted by an amazingly sweet smell, which in turn, evoked another memory.

Stopping dead in her tracks, Emily decided to follow the aroma, which led her to a doughnut stand. This was a new vendor to the mall. They were frying fresh doughnuts and topping them with a simple white syrup. One very strong memory came pouring into her mind as she asked the clerk for one. She still couldn't quite grasp it, but she sat down at a nearby table, closed her eyes and begged the memory to fully emerge and stay.

With the first bite, there it was... a little girl sitting in a kitchen late at night, with a handsome, older man, serving her warm doughnuts just like these. Was this really a memory? *Was this me, and perhaps my father?* Emily thought. It had to be. It didn't make sense that random memories of strangers would just pop into your mind. Convinced that it was a real memory, because she needed it so badly, she smiled, a rarity for her. Something felt real, for the first time in a year.

Completely content to sit with her memory, Emily had no desire to leave the table. And so after she devoured every bite of her doughnut, for the remainder of her two free hours, she didn't move until it was time to walk back to the car. She had always dreaded the trip back to her beautiful, but controlled fortress. This time, though, she would be taking a solid and lovely memory. That one memory would be the solace in the otherwise dismal life that she had been made to believe was real and infinitely inescapable.

When the alarm went off on the timer, Emily gathered her purse and her bag of tea and walked back to the entrance. She saw Bonito standing beside the car, and she instinctively removed the smile from her face before walking through the sliding doors to exit. She had decided to keep her memory and her smile to herself, because she knew Simon would try to convince her that it wasn't real. It was time to put on her poker face.

The trip back home seemed to take less time than it had before. After stepping inside and hearing the piercing sound of the clicking lock on the door, Emily began to walk towards the kitchen to put up her tea. As she did, the mail on the hall table caught her attention. On top of the stack was a colorful travel brochure to an island getaway.

She wasn't supposed to touch the mail, and knowing she was being watched, she didn't pick it up, but the island on the front sparked yet another very strong memory, this time on a boat ride to a tropical island with another young woman. They were both dressed in beautiful gowns and their faces were covered with masquerade masks. This was definitely a memory of a place she'd been before, and recently, but she didn't appear to be destitute, as Simon had given her reason to believe.

Although Emily wasn't sure of the details yet, she was now quite sure that Simon had been lying to her. The memories he had given her were not her own. Her past was coming back to her in random increments. She knew she had to find the truth, but how? He was always watching.

Chapter 1: Perspective

Austin, Texas...

Callie picked up her purse and laptop on the way to the front door, got into her car, and prepared herself for the drudgery of the trip to the courthouse. She'd only been back to work three weeks, but every day since then had been more difficult than the last. So much had changed since she'd been on leave. Her favorite boss, Judge Hamilton, had taken an early retirement because his wife had become ill, and a new judge had been appointed for the two years remaining in the term.

New judges, with the exception of a few, had so much to learn about court procedures, even if they'd been practicing in court for many years. Callie had always been very helpful in the transition because she had so many years of experience with the circuit. The result of her helpfulness had always created a great rapport between her and the judge.

Unfortunately, a substitute reporter was sitting in Callie's chair when Judge Waller took the bench, and the opportunity to create that rapport at the beginning had been missed. Knowing this made it that much more important to Callie to make a good first impression with the judge. In that vein, before her first day back in court, she'd called the judge's court administrator, Becky, to get the inside scoop.

Becky shared what she knew of Judge Waller's likes and dislikes, and Callie decided to go all out and bake the judge's favorite flavor of cupcakes; dark chocolate with peppermint icing. She'd always greeted Judge Hamilton with a hot cup of his favorite blend from Java Joe's, and that had endeared her to him. In Callie's mind, the extra effort put into baking cupcakes would hopefully be the beginning of a great relationship with her new boss.

The cupcakes hadn't gotten the reaction Callie expected, however. It seemed that impressing the only female judge in the district was going to present a much bigger challenge. Judge Waller had politely thanked Callie for the cupcakes, but the thank-you was one similar to what one would say if handed a file. Not to be outdone, Callie decided to up her game. It was built into her personality to be kind, but her dad had taught her the art of winning over any personality type. It had become the most valuable tool in her arsenal.

Callie tried everything she knew to break down the wall Judge Waller had put up, taking a chisel and tapping away, ever so gently. She thought perhaps she would be better off just sticking to helpfulness with regard to the court proceedings. She helped the judge set up her office equipment, started her bench laptop every morning, et cetera. Still, no smile appeared from Judge Waller's beautiful but stern face. Even providing her with rough drafts of transcripts of complex motions hearings proved fruitless.

Nothing was working, and Callie was beginning to struggle. Working with this judge had turned Callie's love of her job into drudgery. The proceedings were a nightmare, with people talking on top of each other constantly and no admonishment from the judge, making Callie's job much more difficult. The one time Callie asked Judge Waller the best way to handle this issue, she was instructed not to interrupt, that the proceedings were being recorded and Callie could fill in the blanks later.

Fill in the blanks? If that was all there was to it, then anyone could do it. Callie knew that wasn't the case, but Judge Waller clearly thought so. This gave Callie cause for concern about her future with this job. She needed to maintain the highest level of professional standards, but the current situation was interfering with her ability to do that. If she couldn't do her job well, she didn't want to do it at all.

She was going to see Dom after work today, so maybe he would have great insight on what she could do to improve her current situation. He was an amazing businessman, and like her dad, he seemed to have a way of winning people over. It had certainly worked with her. She was totally and completely mesmerized by him. Every thought of him made her heart smile.

The drive in to work went from drudgery to calm as Callie's mind took her back to the first time she'd met Dom and all the amazing experiences they'd shared over their several months together. What a rollercoaster ride it had been! From the breathlessness of his romantic gestures, to his arrest for murder and subsequent vindication, followed by an amazing Christmas and New Year's celebration at the ranch, through her recent undercover stint in Puerto Rico which nearly caused her death... it had all been surreal. Her life had turned into a big-screen movie, one she hoped would have an infinite number of sequels.

The time passed without a thought of how she'd gotten to work. Her turn into the courthouse parking lot jolted her back to the present, but the thoughts of Dom had been good for her spirit. If she could claim victory over her battle with the depths of the ocean, no judge on any bench in the world could make her feel less victorious. She would get through the day and come out the other side of it looking beautiful for her date with Dom.

That attitude before work proved to be beneficial, because it had been a difficult day. At 5:00, Callie picked up her things, stopped off at the rest room to freshen up, and walked out to the BMW. She pulled her hair back into a ponytail and put the top down for her drive to the ranch. On her way out of the parking garage, she remembered something she'd told her son when he moved out at 19. Standing in the driveway hugging each other good-bye, Ali had begun to cry. Callie simply said, "Get into your car, drive off and don't look in the rearview mirror, Baby."

Today, she was going to follow her own advice. The stress of the day was in her rearview mirror, and she was leaving it all behind her. It was a beautiful spring day, and the 40-minute drive to the ranch ended up being spectacular. The bluebonnets were beginning to pop up everywhere along the hillsides, and they were more beautiful to see than ever before. The glorious royal blue and white flowers covered the fields as far as the eye could see. Callie always looked forward to their spring arrival every year.

Just after driving through the front gates to Dom's ranch Callie saw a larger patch of bluebonnets, and she couldn't resist the urge to stop and take a photo. After a few gorgeous shots, she got back in her car and went up the drive to the house. *Dom must have been on the tractor today*, she thought to herself. The front pastures had been cut and the baler was waiting in the wings to gather it up for feed.

Dom was feeding the plants as Callie parked and got out of the car. As soon as he heard the car door shut, he turned to smile at Callie and walked over to meet her with his usual strong hug, and a kiss that was worth the 40-minute drive. He always hugged her in a way that felt as if he hadn't seen her in a year. This was one of many things that made him a special man. His kisses made her weak in the knees, so she was grateful for the strong hugs. They were practically the only thing keeping her from falling flat on her face.

As Dom took Callie's hand and walked toward the house, he must have been able to sense that she needed to talk, because he immediately said, "What's on your mind, "Darlin'?"

"Frustrating work stuff, Babe. I could really use your help with something."

"Whatever I can do, you know I will. But first, a glass of wine. I've got a bottle waiting on the patio for us."

"A glass of wine by the pool with my gorgeous Cowboy? Who could say no to that?" Callie responded, giving Dom a beautiful smile.

Dom gave Callie's hand a little squeeze, opening the door for her as they went inside. Callie put her purse on the kitchen counter, and Dom went to get cleaned up from the gardening. Out of the corner of her eye, Callie noticed something different about the patio. She could only see a glimpse of it from where she was standing, so she stepped towards it to get the full view.

The sun had begun to fade, and Callie stood in front of the sliding glass door to the patio, watching in amazement as the flickering lights from the candles danced almost in tune with the soft jazz music playing on the patio speakers. Candles in every size surrounded the patio and lit a path around the pool. Dom had mentioned wine and glasses, but he had failed to mention all of the beautiful accompaniments. The attention to detail was truly Dom. Her cowboy never failed to surprise her with his romantic prowess. He knew exactly how to set the tone for an evening with her; it seemed to come naturally to him. Even though he'd been this way throughout the entirety of their relationship, it never got old.

Completely entranced by the soothing environment, Callie hadn't heard Dom walk up behind her, so she was a little startled by his soft embrace around her waist.

"You scared me!" Callie said, giggling.

"I'm sorry, Darlin'. You must have been another world away."

"Yes, in this beautiful world you created. Life with you is such a blessing. I'm not sure how you always know what I need before I do, but..."

"A cowboy never tells his secrets," Dom replied, giving Callie his sexy little wink. "Seriously, though, you are the most natural woman I've ever known. Your open heart and gentle spirit allow me to be the man God intended for you."

Those words poured over Callie like honey on a warm buttermilk biscuit. She'd been alone for so long after Mike's death, and she had been content with that; but from the very moment that Dom asked to share a lakeside view of the sunset with her, she was hooked. He was everything she never knew she wanted, and now, she couldn't imagine a future without him.

Callie took a minute to totally immerse herself in Dom's words and then said, "Babe, I love you more than I ever thought possible. I've never been prouder to call a man my own than I am right this minute. Your words are intoxicating," Callie responded. "Who needs wine? It would just muddy everything up."

"Well, it's already chilled, but I can put it away if you want."

"No way! It would detract from the entire experience you created for me. Let's get this rodeo started!"

Callie took the liberty of pouring the wine, which was followed by a clinking of their two glasses in silence. There was no need for words, because the toast had really already been given. Sealing things finally with a warm kiss, they grabbed the bottle of wine, took off their shoes, sat down on the concrete deck of the pool and put their toes into the warm water.

It was at that point that Dom encouraged Callie to talk to him about what was going on with work. She shared her struggles with her new judge as Dom listened quietly. He was a great listener, never interrupting until he was invited. After a lengthy career as a court reporter, listening to others without participating in the conversation had become second nature for Callie. Most of the people in Callie's life didn't understand her need to talk things out -- well, to talk, period -- but Dom certainly did.

When Callie finished sharing what her plight was, she asked, "So what do you think, Babe? How can I win her over?"

Dom responded with pure resolve and a serious face. "Darlin', some horses aren't meant for you to tame. Maybe it's time to find another horse."

Surprisingly, Callie understood exactly what he meant. She'd been looking at this as if she had no other opportunities, that this was her one and only option. Because of her skill, experience, work ethic and certifications, she had made herself highly marketable. Suddenly, the stress of feeling defeated melted away like the wax underneath a candle's flame.

She smiled at Dom, leaned over and kissed him again and thanked him for opening her eyes to all the possibilities the future could hold for her. Now refreshed and relaxed, she could just be in the moment with her cowboy. She could think about the possibilities tomorrow. For now, it was time to stop and smell the roses, and they never smelled sweeter.

The cool breeze started to get a little brisk, so Dom took that cue and lit a fire in the outdoor fireplace nearby. They both agreed that they were getting hungry, and while Callie made a trip to the bathroom, Dom took the shish kabobs out of the fridge to let them come to room temperature and went back outside to fire up the grill. The baked sweet potatoes already smelled amazing in the oven, and it wouldn't be long until they were ready to devour.

As Callie came out of the bathroom, she checked her phone. There were no messages, but she then remembered the pictures she'd taken of the bluebonnets. She pulled them up to look at them again just as Dom came back into the kitchen.

"Anything important?" Dom asked.

"Babe, you have to see these gorgeous pictures I took of the bluebonnets up front when I came in earlier! Look how beautiful they are."

Dom took the phone from Callie and said, "I've been so busy cutting pastures today that I didn't even notice how much they'd grown. They're really special this year, huh? I threw a couple thousand extra seeds out this year to highlight the front entry. So you like them?"

"Are you kidding me? I love them! I look forward to seeing them when spring arrives every year. They're just breathtaking! They give me a sense of bright days ahead, if that makes sense."

"I'd never thought about it quite that way, but now that you point it out, it makes perfect sense. Looking at them makes your smile extra sparkly."

"That's my new lip balm, silly."

"Oh!" Dom responded, and then they both began to laugh.

With that, they moved back out to the patio grill and poured another glass of wine. The fire added yet another warm glow to the patio paradise, and looking up to the skies, Callie could see it was the clearest night she had seen so far this year. The moon was sitting high in the sky, and away from the lights of the city, the stars were glistening in unison with the candlelight.

Pure heaven, Callie thought. A quick glance over her shoulder to search for her favorite two stars in the sky showed that they were as bright as they ever had been, letting her know they were still watching over her. Logically, of course, she knew they weren't really her daddy and Mike, but it gave her such joy to imagine that they were.

Feeling Dom's eyes on her, she quickly met his gaze and noticed a huge grin on his face, as if he knew a big secret. She smiled at him girlishly, almost blushing, and said, "What?"

"Just watching my lady glow," he said. "The kabobs are ready when you are. Ready?"

"I'm starving. I'll get the platter and set the table."

"Perfect," Dom replied.

In half an hour dinner was over and Callie was feeling relaxed but exhausted, having been wined and dined after a long day in court. She thought Dom must have been feeling the same after a long day in the pastures, and because there would be another long one the following morning, they agreed to clean the kitchen, set the coffee pot timer and go to bed early. Ordinarily, Callie would have driven home, but there was no way she would risk a 45-minute drive on dark, winding roads after two glasses of wine.

With the two of them together working on kitchen duty, the task was finished in about 15 minutes, at which point Dom took Callie by the hand to get ready for bed. He handed Callie the old rodeo T-shirt that she loved to wear when she slept over, and she changed and got into bed. She was so worn out that she didn't even feel Dom get into bed next to her.

Sometime later...

The water felt cold against Callie's skin, and the quiet was deafening. She was paralyzed, unable to control her descent. *Why can't I move?* It was dark, and Callie was afraid. She could feel the fingers of death reaching out to her as her lungs became heavier and heavier. *Help me! Somebody, please, help me!* But no one was here. As she began to feel the life being pulled from her body and her last breath upon her...

Callie gasped for breath and sat straight up in the bed, Dom's gentle arms immediately around her. "Darlin', it's okay. I'm here. You're safe now. It was just a dream."

"Oh, Dom!" Callie said, taking a deep breath, "I thought I was drowning. I couldn't breathe, I couldn't move, I couldn't do anything."

"I thought these nightmares had stopped, Callie."

"They haven't, but I didn't want to worry you, Babe."

"It's perfectly natural to have flashbacks like this for some time, but I can't help you with them if you're not honest with me about them. How about you let me decide what to worry about? We definitely need to talk about this, because you can't share this particular experience with anyone except a CIA shrink."

"I know you're right," Callie said. "I was just hoping they would just stop on their own."

"That's not the way this works, Darlin'. I'm going to get some water for you. Maybe you can get back to sleep."

"It's nearly 4:00 anyway. The alarm will be going off in about an hour, so there's really no point. I might as well get up and start my day. You go back to sleep, though. At least one of us should get a little rest. I'm sorry I woke you, Babe."

"And I'm glad I was here to hold you. But if you're up, I'm up. That's the deal," Dom insisted. "We're a team, right?"

"Of course."

"All right, then. I'll get the coffee going. You get your shower, and breakfast will be waiting on the bar for you. I love you, Darlin'."

"I love you too, Babe."

Twenty-five minutes later, Callie walked into the kitchen, and Dom had breakfast laid out on the bar. Fresh-squeezed orange juice, coffee with vanilla caramel creamer, just the way Callie liked it, and chocolate-chip pancakes with blueberry syrup from the farm next door.

"I thought you needed some chocolate to start your day," Dom said, smiling at Callie.

"You have my heart, Babe, in every way I know how to give it."

In the dark of the morning, Callie and Dom began to recount their experience in Puerto Rico. Dom had many years of undercover experience under his belt, but Callie, being a novice, had no idea the impact a near-death experience would have on her psyche. She knew it was important to deal with it, and she was grateful that she had Dom to guide her through the painful process.

It was no small feat to have taken down a federal judge who orchestrated a sex trafficking ring. Callie was really proud of her role in that, especially because it involved helping one of his victims, Mercedes, begin a new life. But being knocked into the ocean during a storm was more than she'd bargained for. And the judge's wife, Ingrid, the true mastermind of the organization, was still at large. Dom thought this may be one of the reasons Callie's nightmares continued to haunt her.

Callie knew she was extremely lucky to have been found by the kind doctor, Tom, who had been trying to investigate the ring, and had been watching as she was taken down into the current. Thinking about that brought Callie's mind back to his life-saving efforts and the enormous debt of gratitude she owed him.

"I can't get Tom off my mind, Babe. If it weren't for him, we wouldn't be sitting here having this conversation. I can't help but think about how desperate he must be to find his daughter. I know that we agreed to wait, but..."

"I'm way ahead of you, Darlin'. I have some feelers out there. I'm just waiting for some phone calls. When I know, you'll know. Okay?"

"I should have known you'd be on top of things. You haven't broken a promise yet. Maybe one day I'll trust that you're always thinking of me."

"Trust is built, brick by brick. We're going to have a mansion one day," Dom said.

Feeling much better after her conversation with Dom, Callie looked up and saw that the light from the day had already started without her noticing. She glanced at her watch and realized it was almost time to leave for work. She helped Dom gather up the dishes and tidy up the kitchen, thinking that she couldn't envision a better way to start her day.

"I'd better get started. Today is Friday, and we have docket call. I want to get there early. The last 12 hours with you have been amazing, with one exception," Callie said.

"Really? Something wrong, Darlin'?"

"The 12 hours is up, and I have to leave."

"I'll keep your spot warm for you," Dom said.

"Thanks, Babe. I'll see you tonight at my place?"

"Count on it," he replied.

Dom walked Callie out to her car, gave her a huge hug and kiss, closed the door once she was belted in, and stood there watching as she drove off. She couldn't resist the urge to look in her rearview mirror this time, because this was going to be her future. She could feel it. There wasn't a finer sight to see. That would be the thing that would get her through another court day with her new judge.

She got to the courthouse in plenty of time to get set up and ready for her day. *Bring it on, Judge Waller. I'll take everything you throw at me today.* The can-do attitude turned out to be Callie's best plan of attack, because there was request after request for testimony to be read back, following a full day of interruptions, and no break except a 30-minute lunch break. Callie came out triumphant at the end of the day, and seeing the judge in the hallway on her way out, smiled blissfully and said, "Have a great weekend, Judge. See you bright and early Monday morning."

The judge paused and gave Callie a puzzled look, adding a hesitant, "Okay." Callie sort of snickered to herself on her way to the parking garage, because the chains were now unshackled. Callie had options, and there was something so powerful about that knowledge. She didn't need to share it. It would make no difference to Judge Waller anyway, because she didn't care who sat in that chair; she placed no value on the person or the skill. Dom was right; this horse wasn't for Callie to tame. It was time for a change.

On the way home, she decided to stop by the market to pick up a few things for a special dinner to thank Dom. Grilled salmon with a brown sugar and mustard glaze with a side of saffron rice sounded great; and for dessert, an Earl Grey chocolate torte with a raspberry drizzle. She'd already made the cake the week before and frozen it, so it only needed thawing out for a half hour.

The trip to the market was a quick one, so Callie made it home in plenty of time for a quick shower. Afterwards she changed into her favorite pair of jeans, a halter covered by a light sweater and, of course, her one-of-a-kind red boots that had been gifted to her by Dom. A spritz of his favorite perfume, a tap of the phone to get a little Josh Turner on, and she was ready to get dinner going.

Dom gave a short knock on the door and walked in, and Callie said, "Hey, in the kitchen, Cowboy!" Dom put a bag of fresh basil from the garden on the counter, and Callie leaned in to give him a welcome kiss.

"Dinner smells amazing. What's on the menu tonight?" asked Dom, peering into the oven.

"Salmon and rice. I hope you're hungry. As usual, I made enough for an army. I really need to learn how to cook for two at some point, I guess."

"Why would you want to do that? Everything you make is worth eating at least three times."

Callie grinned and said, "Aww, what a sweet thing to say. I knew I kept you around for some reason."

"Is there anything I can do to help, Darlin'?"

"Well, you could taste this raspberry sauce and tell me what you think."

"Happy to," Dom said, leaning in to what Callie thought was a kiss on the cheek, but it was a little more than a peck, as if he was glued there.

"What are you doing?" Callie asked.

"Tasting the raspberry sauce. You had some on your cheek. It's perfect," he said.

"Oh, my God! Why didn't you tell me?!"

"I thought maybe you had a plan for it there. Who am I to second-guess the smartest woman I know?"

"For that, you'll get extra dessert. But you knew that, didn't you?"

Dom simply raised his eyebrows and sheepishly grinned as if he had a secret he wasn't telling. Callie put the final touches on the salmon while Dom set the table, and the two sat down to eat. Dom seemed to love the meal, because he got up to get seconds. Callie's plate was empty and she was full, so as Dom continued eating, she began to talk to him about her new attitude about Judge Waller and how much she appreciated the advice he'd given her; that it really had opened her eyes to exciting opportunities.

"I'm going to give Pam a call in the morning. She's been begging me for years to be her deposition reporter. She has plenty of work, both here and in San Antonio, and since she's my best friend, I don't have to worry about getting paid. I can take what I want, make more money and work less hours. I can take my retirement and stay on the county's health insurance. I think this is going to be a blessing, and I have you to thank for yet another one of those."

Dom looked up from his salmon and said, "Darlin', the real blessing is having a partner who trusts you enough to ask for help. I know how hard that is for an independent woman."

Callie got up to take Dom's plate after he finished his last bite, and put the dishes in the sink. There was still a little daylight left, so they decided to take a walk down to the trails at the back of the neighborhood to burn off some of the calories. The weeds had been cut down recently, making the trails clear enough to venture down to the small pond.

After the ten-minute brisk walk to the pond, Dom pointed out a large pair of pine tree stumps for the two of them to sit and enjoy the quietness of the still, murky water. As they sat and looked out into the pond, they could see little air bubbles popping up at the surface, indicating life beneath it. Dusk was on the horizon, so they wouldn't be staying long, but Callie noticed a beautiful old oak tree about a hundred yards to the right of where they were sitting and commented on its beauty.

Dom got up and walked over to snap a shot of the old beauty with his smartphone. Callie got up and started back up the trail, but then noticed Dom retrieve his pocket knife and stopped to see what he was doing with the knife. There was about a six-inch bare spot in the bark about five feet up from the ground, and Dom started to carve into it.

"What's up, Babe?"

"Letting future generations know that I love you," Dom said. "The bare wood seemed to be inviting it."

When he was finished and moved his hands, Callie saw that the carving looked similar to one she'd seen in junior high. He'd carved their initials on either side of a yin-yang symbol. This was something as original as Dom, and it was far more meaningful than a heart would have been.

Callie looked over at Dom as he was admiring his work. He had the cutest little-boy smile on his face. She hugged him from behind and gave him a kiss on the back of his shoulder blade, adding, "That is just about the sweetest thing ever. Revisiting our youth, are we?"

Dom responded, "I wouldn't go near a girl when I was that age. They scared the daylights out of me. But you make me feel like a 13-year-old, so it's like starting all over again, only with money."

"Funny... I thought I was the only one of us who felt that way. Isn't it a great feeling?"

"The best, Darlin'. The very best."

Dom turned around, wrapped his arms around her tightly, kissed her passionately, and then memorialized the moment with a snapshot of the two of them standing in front of Dom's expression of love. It was getting a little darker at that point, so they made their way back up the trail to the main road and walked back to the house.

"Are you ready for dessert?" Callie asked, walking towards the kitchen.

"Is that a rhetorical question?" Dom replied. "That walk made me hungry again."

Callie couldn't help chuckling out loud, because Dom was always ready for dessert. His sweet tooth matched Callie's, calorie for calorie, except Callie had to work much harder to fight the urge to indulge it. The cake was already thawed, and the sauce was covered and left on warm on the stovetop while they were gone. As she served the plates, she added just a dollop of fresh whipped cream to each, and they retreated to the patio to enjoy what was left of the evening together.

In talking about their plans for the following day, Dom mentioned that he had to head back to the ranch later because the following morning there were several head of cattle being delivered, and he needed to be sure that all of them were healthy before signing for them. Callie said that she would use the time to sleep in and maybe have lunch with Pam to talk over her plan to freelance.

An hour later, Callie walked with Dom out to his truck and kissed him goodnight. She walked back into the house and went upstairs to soak in a hot tub filled with jasmine in the hopes of getting good sleep and bypassing the nightmares at least for one night. The jasmine proved to be a really nice help in relaxing her, because after her nightly regimen of prayers, she was quickly off to sleep.

The nightmares were of no consequence, if they happened at all, because Callie woke up completely refreshed the following morning, having no memory of any hint of interrupted sleep. She had even been able to sleep an extra hour, finally getting out of bed at around 9:00. She poured her first cup of coffee, read the Saturday paper and picked up the phone to call Pam.

The two of them spent a few minutes catching up, and Pam was excited to hear about the prospect of Callie's exodus from the courtroom. They agreed to meet for lunch and a little girl time around noon, and after hanging up, Callie got out her computer and began to put a financial plan in place. She just wanted a clear picture of her budget before talking to Pam and making any final decisions.

Once that was done, she got dressed and ready for the day with Pam and left the house. They'd decided to meet at a new teahouse, a sweet little out-of-the-way spot between Austin and San Antonio, for a light lunch and a pot of tea. Time with Pam was always delightful. She had always been on Callie's side, no matter what.

Seeing Pam waiting outside for her, she quickly parked and ran over to give her a huge hug. It had been weeks since Callie had seen her, and she was anxious to catch up. Once the two got seated at a table and ordered drinks and lunch, their conversation took off at its normal fast pace.

"So tell me... how are you? How's Dom? What prompted this big move, and when can I schedule you for a depo?"

"Geez, Pam, come up for air. Ha ha! I'm fine, and Dom's better than ever. He's been taking really good care of me since we got back from San Juan."

"He's really a great guy, Callie. We weren't always sure about that, were we?"

"Not when he showed up on my docket for murder and then I found out he was a spy and I couldn't talk to him. That was fun, right?"

The two of them laughed, looking back at it all, and then the conversation turned to the reason for Callie's decision to leave her official position. Callie laid it all out, and Pam understood. She said she'd heard about Judge Waller, explaining that she'd had similar experiences with a few other judges in San Antonio during her career.

They talked through lunch, and when it was over, Callie had made her decision. Working with Pam was going to be a great change in her life. Taking the bull by the horns and wrestling it to the ground was going to be a far better idea than having it twist and turn furiously and then toss Callie's flailing, helpless body into the dirt.

The two hugged good-bye, agreeing to stay in touch as the process unfolded, and Callie decided that she was going home to take an afternoon walk followed by an afternoon nap. There were no transcripts on her agenda since she'd been off for nearly two months with the Puerto Rico project, and on Monday, she'd be giving her two-week notice. She'd normally have given a month, but she already knew the young reporter who replaced her during her absence would be more than willing to jump into her chair at the slightest mention of an opportunity.

With that in mind, she decided that after her nap, she'd place the call to that reporter and give her a heads-up so that when Callie gave her notice, she could give them her recommended replacement. Judge Waller and the horrible record in her courtroom would then become someone else's horse to tame.

The lovely, relaxing weekend with Dom was soon over, and armed with her letter of resignation, Callie decided to get to the courthouse much earlier than she had since her return from Puerto Rico. This time, she was actually looking forward to getting the letter in the judge's hands quickly and moving forward with her new life plan.

Judge Waller, as Callie had predicted, had little reaction to the letter, thanked her for her service, and promptly asked if there was anything else she needed. Callie simply responded, "No, Ma'am. That's it. Thank you for making this easy for me." Of course, Callie was referring to the ease of the decision, but worded it in a way that would appease the judge's ego. She rarely burned bridges, and there was no need to do that now.

The rest of the week was uneventful, until Friday. Judge Waller called her into her office to let her know that the new reporter would be starting on Monday and that Callie was free from her service to the county. Although this news came as a little bit of a surprise to Callie, she decided it was a blessing in disguise. She'd only given her notice out of courtesy anyway. She was raised not to overstay her welcome, so she gracefully gave the judge a polite thank-you and went to her office to gather a few final personal belongings.

She called Dom on her way out to her car and let him know what had happened. He said, "Darlin', I think that confirms that you made the right choice, don't you? Don't give it another thought. That's in your rearview mirror, right?"

"I couldn't have said it better myself, Babe. I'll see you in about 45 minutes. It's time to celebrate the next chapter."

"That's right."

Callie hung up the phone and put the top down again. It was time to smell those roses. Leaving the courthouse for the last time was bittersweet, but the delight of what was in front of her simply tipped the scales over the history of her career in this courthouse. She would remember the wonderful judges and colleagues who made her days brighter as she dealt with Mike's death. She'd reach out to them over the next week to say a proper good-bye and thank them for making her life sweeter.

The drive out to the ranch seemed different this time, but Callie knew that it was more than likely because she was different. It had nothing to do with the scenery; it was her perception of the scenery. It was only more beautiful because she appreciated its beauty more today than she had yesterday. *Okay, silly,* she thought, *Stop the self-analysis and go get your cowboy!*

Arriving at the ranch, that's exactly what she did. She got out and burst through the front door, running over to Dom and jumping into his waiting arms, shouting, "I'm free!"

Dom laughed, responding, "No, Darlin', never free. You're available. Free is a nasty word for a business owner."

Callie laughed uncontrollably as Dom gently lowered her feet down onto the floor. And then he began to talk to her about his day. He'd gotten a phone call from one of his sources in France, giving him a lead on Tom's daughter, Emily. Callie's smiling face turned to a serious one at this point, listening intently as Dom went over the details of the call. Her sleuth radar had suddenly kicked in.

"So should we call Tom?" Callie asked.

"Oh, I already called him just a little while ago."

"You did?"

"Yeah, sure. Did you not want me to?"

"Well, yes, but I thought it would be a conference call. We both agreed to help him, right?"

"Oh, Darlin', after everything you went through on the island, I'm really worried about you getting involved with this."

For the first time in a long time, Callie was feeling something other than adoration for Dom. He must have seen her altered demeanor, because he tried to explain further, but it was too late. Callie's independence made itself known right away.

"Okay. So here's the deal, Babe. You don't want me to keep things from you that are bothering me, right? So I'm telling you straight out that I love you for being worried about me, but it was my life that Tom saved, and I owe him the debt. You're my partner, and I need you to trust me as a partner, not just your partner in love, but your partner in life. Are we on the same page?"

Dom was quiet for a little longer than Callie was comfortable with, so she reached up and caressed the side of his face. When she did, he relaxed, looked into her eyes and said,

"This is what I love most about you. You said you loved me before you told me how much I screwed up. Partnering in undercover work is really hard when you love somebody, which is why they don't allow fraternization in police work.

"But I know how much this means to you, and I also know that when I was in trouble, I trusted you enough to get me out of it. I'm so sorry, Darlin'. I wanted to protect you and I forgot to respect you."

Callie smiled up at him and said, "Apology accepted, but now you owe me a treat. I'm thinking a pricy bottle of champagne is in order."

"Deal!"

Dom went down to the wine cellar and brought back up a bottle of Dom Perignon, popped the cork and toasted to their newfound partnership. They then sat down at the bar and began to chart their course for the plan to find Emily and return her to her father.

Chapter 2: Partnership Redefined

San Juan, Puerto Rico...

The water is unusually still today, Tom thought to himself while sitting down on the beach near the spot he'd found Callie. When he got the call from Dom the day before, he couldn't believe his ears. Since Franco's private island had been virtually shut down by federal agents just a few months before, there weren't any signs of life coming from it, and Tom had begun to lose all hope of finding Emily.

He'd thought about leaving San Juan, but he couldn't bear the thought of returning home without his precious daughter. From the day Emily was born, he understood what it meant to love without limits. His beautiful wife had been taken from him when Emily was only five, and from that point forward, she had been his only focus.

Staring into the clear, blue-green water, Tom remembered the first time he took Emily to the beach. It was shortly after her mother had passed away, and they were both really missing her, so Tom decided to pack up the car and drive to Pensacola for the day. They stopped for breakfast at Denny's on the way down from their hometown of Evergreen, Alabama, but Emily ate very little of her pancakes, insisting she wasn't hungry. Tom knew she really just wanted to get to the beach.

When they finally parked, the smile on Emily's face was worth the lack of sleep that Tom had gotten coming off his shift at the hospital ER the night before. He took her down to the water, armed with everything they needed for the day, and off Emily ran. Tom could barely keep up with her little body and cautioned her to wait for him.

He dropped his armful of towels, ice chest and toys, and grabbed the sunscreen, coating Emily with it. She was blonde and fair-skinned, so 20 minutes in the sun without sunscreen would ruin the day. After that was done, Emily tugged at his hand and said, "Okay, okay, Daddy, come on! Let's get this show on the road!"

Tom was so thrilled to see that sweet little smile on her face that he quickly said, "Okay, Baby. First one to the water is a rotten egg." Of course, he let Emily win, but as soon as she got her feet wet, a wave came crashing into her and knocked her down, and she began to scream and cry.

Rushing to quickly scoop her up into his arms, Tom told her that it was okay, daddy was there, and as long as he was living, he would always keep her safe. Her sobbing dried up as soon as he began to splash around with her in the water. It was one of his best memories of time with Emily.

The beautiful memories of that joyful day with Emily quickly turned to guilt and anxiety as he thought about the fact that he hadn't been able to protect her. He'd signed off on her trip to Puerto Rico, never realizing she could just disappear. The notification from the local police was the most horrific phone call he'd ever received, and it had broken his heart to think that he might never see her sweet smile again. She'd been gone for nearly 15 months now. Would they ever find her?

Just as he began to travel down that depressing road in his mind again, his cell phone rang. He looked at it to see that it was Callie and was grateful for the welcome distraction. Answering immediately, he said, "Hey there! How's my beautiful patient?"

"Full of life and happiness, thanks to you. How are you, my friend? Dom told me he'd updated you on the new lead on your daughter, but I wanted to touch base with you myself to let you know we've put a plan together to help you find her. We're going to track down every lead."

"So you're in on the case too? Dom had mentioned that he'd be doing this solo."

Callie paused briefly and said, "Yeah, well, my cowboy got a little ahead of himself on that, but we're all square now."

"He wasn't real keen on my participation either, but if you're looking for my daughter, I'm not staying behind again to wait for news. Besides, I'm a doctor, and somebody may need medical care."

"I understand, Tom. Dom and I both have children, and I'm sure we'd feel exactly the same as you under the same set of circumstances. We should be there sometime in the next few days. We'll give you a call with the details when the flight is confirmed. Someone's at my door, so let me see what that's about."

"Okay, Callie. Thank you, from the bottom of my heart. You've given me hope again. I'll be ready to leave when you get here. It was so good to hear your voice again."

"You too, Tom. We'll talk to you soon."

Tom set his phone back down beside him on the beach towel, and he looked up into the skies and said a small prayer of thanks for the kindness of strangers. He would have to hope that this would end with Emily's safe return.

Callie's house...

Callie opened the door to an unexpected delivery from the local delivery lady. She hadn't seen the lady in a while, and she was all smiles as she saw Callie and asked her to sign for the package. They exchanged pleasantries while she was signing for the box, and after thanking her, she closed the door behind her and walked over to the sofa. The return address on the box wasn't familiar to her, so she opened the box to see what was inside.

Once the packing paper and Bubble Wrap were out of the way, she could see that there was a card with a small ring box inside. She opened the card first, and once again, Dom had surprised her. The handwritten card simply read, "My humble attempt at rekindling our special partnership." Callie pressed the card to her lips to give it a light kiss, as if Dom were standing there. He was such a special man, and she felt so lucky to have found him.

She put the card down onto her lap and picked up the box to open it. Inside was another truly original design. Callie had never asked Dom, but she was certain that he had a jewelry designer on standby 24/7, because everything he'd given her was a work of art.

This ring had a medium-width band with a yin-yang symbol on top. The black side was made of onyx, and the white side was the most beautiful mother of pearl she'd ever seen. But the one thing that made this piece special was the initials set into the stones. The D sat at the top of the white side, and the C sat at the bottom of the black side, joining into each other and aligning with the curves separating the two halves.

Callie took it out of the box and put it on her middle finger, and it fit perfectly. She picked up the phone and was about to call Dom, but the doorbell rang again. She got up to answer the door, and it was him, standing there with a fresh cup of coffee and what appeared to be Danish from the bakery down the road.

Curious as to what he was doing there at 10:00 in the morning, she said, "I thought you had a meeting at the ranch?"

"I did, but I finished up earlier than expected and thought I'd surprise you."

"Well, that wasn't the only surprise from you that I got this morning, Cowboy. You didn't have to do that, but I absolutely love it! It's almost as special as you. But how did you get this beauty done so fast? We just had our partnership conversation last night."

"Darlin', an undercover agent never tells his secrets, but because we're partners, I can trust you. I had this designed just after I carved it into the tree. It just seemed timely to give it to you today. Some things come as a total surprise to even the best planners."

They kissed in the doorway, and when Callie reached to take the bakery bag from Dom, she noticed something new on his finger. She held his hand as she turned it over to see what was there and found a ring nearly identical to hers, except the band was wider and the top was thicker.

Noticing that she was intrigued by it, he said, "We're equal partners, right? So I figured there wasn't a better way to signify that than to wear identical rings. Mine's just more manly than yours."

"Ha! Well, that makes perfect sense, because you're definitely a manly man. Beautiful, but manly," Callie said, winking and then letting out a chuckle as she went to the kitchen to get a couple of plates for the Danish.

Dom followed her into the kitchen and they began to dig in to the apple-cinnamon Danish as Callie relayed her recent call with Tom. Dom told Callie that he'd gotten word from his contact in D.C. that Emily's case was still open, but the trail had gone cold. Dom had asked if he and Callie could be put on special assignment to follow the lead Dom had turned up through his own sources, and after speaking with the agent in charge of Emily's case, the request was approved.

The government jet and all its resources would be made available to them, conditional upon keeping the agent informed every step of the way. Dom told Callie that he thought it would be best to keep quiet about Tom's involvement in the investigation, because he knew that the government would frown on it. Callie agreed, and they both decided that Tom's involvement would be limited. They would give him something to do in order to keep him busy and allow him to feel useful, but that would be the extent of it because his lack of training and emotional connection to the case could put everyone in harm's way.

The jet was scheduled to arrive at a private strip at the Austin airport on Tuesday morning, and since Callie lived closer, they decided that it would be best for Dom to spend Monday night at her place. They would lay over in San Juan with Tom for a day, refuel, and then the three of them would leave for Alsace, France first thing on Wednesday. It was about a 15-hour flight from San Juan, bypassing U.S. Customs, and with the time difference, that should put them down at Basel-Mulhouse Airport in Upper Alsace sometime mid to late afternoon on Thursday.

With only a few days to prepare for the trip, Dom left for the ranch to get things squared away before they left. Callie had no idea how long they'd be gone, but Dom's advice had been for her to pack light and buy whatever she needed later, taking along an empty suitcase inside a smaller one.

The packing went much faster than Callie had imagined, which left plenty of time for a trip to the grocery store to pick up a few snacks. While she was there, she decided she'd grab a few ingredients to bake a few of her special treats. It was time to surprise her cowboy. He wasn't the only one who could pull off a little coup.

The grocery store was packed, but Callie just needed a few items. Because of that and opting for the self-check line, she was in and out in 15 minutes. When she got back home, the eggs she'd laid out on the counter were room temperature and ready to add to her recipes. She turned the oven on and got the sweet sounds of Harry Connick, Jr. going on her iPad, and the stage was set to unwind and create.

As her hands began to play with the dough for her grandma's homemade egg noodles, her mind began to drift back to her family sitting around the table after church on Sundays. She remembered the love around the table, the jokes that were told, and the embarrassing moments that made her family unique to her. She laughed out loud as she remembered a particular occasion.

Grandma's chicken and noodles were always asked for and never turned down, and were complemented by amazing mashed potatoes, Aunt Nellie's to-die-for macaroni and cheese and something green, of course. The green veggie could change, but the rest was a necessity. On that particular Sunday afternoon, the entire family was sitting around the oval table in the dining room, and the food had been served. Grandma had just finished the prayer, when she sneezed. And bless her heart, when she did, her dentures flew out of her mouth and across the table, landing right in the middle of Callie's dad's mashed potatoes.

The horrified look on everyone's face was indescribable. Callie, her brothers and her cousins were all teenagers at the time, and they all knew better than to laugh, since they certainly didn't want to embarrass their sweet grandma. But the surprise of seeing the flying teeth and the look of astonishment on Callie's dad's face was almost too much to bear.

Callie's dad, in his usual and brilliant way of making an awkward moment seem as if it had been planned, simply looked up from his plate and said, "Mom, if you wanted a bite of my potatoes, all you had to do was ask." Then there was laughter like no laughter that had ever appeared at that table. Permission had been given to laugh, and it was a memory that had made Callie laugh no matter how many times it came back around.

While lost in her thoughts, Callie had kneaded the dough sufficiently, so she laid the dough onto the table, rolled it out paper thin, threw extra flour on top, and left it to dry for three hours while she began to bake up an assortment of cookies and Dom's favorite brownie recipe.

Just as she stepped away from the table, the trip to Alsace popped back into her mind. *Wait a minute*, she thought to herself, *we're going to Alsace! That's where my family originated!* She remembered studying a little of her family tree many years before, but due to the seriousness of the upcoming mission, the thought hadn't occurred to her that she would be visiting the place of her heritage, something that her dad had always wanted to do.

It was such a surreal feeling that Callie didn't quite know what to do with it. She immediately got cold chills, which were quickly followed by a warm feeling in her soul and a smile on her face. "Daddy, I'm taking you with me," she said out loud. She couldn't wait to share this recent realization with Dom, along with the surprising culinary delights she had in store for him when he returned on Monday night.

The cookies and brownies were finished and cooling on the counter just in time for Callie to roll up the noodle dough and cut into thin strips. She'd made a full batch, so she put a bag in the fridge for Monday and three bags into the freezer. Then she packaged up the sweet treats in airtight containers and sat down on the patio with some wine, fruit and cheese, deciding to give the kids a call. This time she could tell them where she was going and what she was doing, and why.

She'd just talked to Ali two weeks before, but Lauren was just getting in from an article assignment in Kenya. Lauren was her first call, and once they talked about the excitement of Lauren's trip, she shared her news with her. Of course, Lauren was concerned, but she understood why it was so important to her mom and begged her to be careful. They said their "I love yous," and Callie promised to check in via text message when she could.

The call to Ali was a little more difficult. He had been more protective over Callie since his dad passed away, and he wasn't a fan of her undercover work because it put her life in jeopardy. Callie reassured him that Dom would be by her side, which calmed his fears slightly, but he still wasn't happy about it and insisted she check in frequently.

Callie agreed and asked him to put Michael and Sophia on the phone, which served two purposes: One, it gave Callie an excuse to change the topic; and two, it gave her the warm and fuzzy feeling she needed from hearing the sounds of joy from their sweet voices when they talked to her.

Hanging up the phone, she was filled with exuberance over the upcoming covert joint mission with Dom. She'd never really seen him in the field; the only time had been the few minutes when he'd attempted to rescue her from Franco's island, before he was struck from behind and knocked out. This time, they were starting the mission together and would see it to its fruition.

Her thoughts about Dom made her miss him, so she decided to take a drive out to the ranch to see him. She thought that maybe she could burn off some of her excess energy by helping him get ready for the trip. She took out a few brownies and put them in a baggie, slipped them into her purse, grabbed the keys, and set out for the ranch.

When she got there, one of the hands told her that Dom was out in the stables feeding the horses. *Oh, perfect timing for a ride,* she thought. She hadn't ridden DD in a week or so, and a brisk ride was just what she needed. She walked over to the stables, and seeing Dom brushing DD, she walked up behind him and gave him a huge hug. He turned to see her standing there, and his eyes lit up like a little boy looking into a toy store window.

"Hey, Darlin'! You sure know how to make a man smile after a hard day's work. What a wonderful surprise!"

"I finished up what I was doing at the house, and I missed you. I'm nursing some nervous energy, and I thought I might work some of it off with a ride. Are you game?"

"Sure! I just finished grooming our babies. Let's get them saddled up and take a fast ride down to the back pasture. They really need the exercise anyway."

The ride took the edge off for both of them. Dom hadn't said much about the trip other than the business end of the mission, but Callie knew that having her along was putting extra pressure on him. She was going to do everything she could to show him that his worry was unnecessary.

After trotting back to the stables and putting DD and Yin-Yang down for the night, Dom and Callie decided to grab their suits and get into the Jacuzzi. The sun was just starting to set on the Austin horizon, and the temperature had begun to cool, making the warmth of the hot tub comfortable and cozy. Callie was sitting in front of Dom on the concrete bench, totally enveloped by his arms and legs. They were both feeling completely relaxed, and Callie shared her comical grandma memory, along with her revelation about Alsace and her heritage.

Dom laughed so hard that he nearly pushed Callie out of his lap. He said, "That's the most hilarious story I've ever heard! I can almost see it through your eyes. I wish I could have met your dad, Darlin'. I would have told him what a fine job he did raising such an amazing woman."

"You would have impressed him with your handshake, but you would have sealed the deal with that comment," Callie responded.

"And the fact that we're going to walk in perhaps the same footsteps as your ancestors is a very cool thing. Even though this is a business trip, I promise to take you back there one day so that we can really explore."

Callie was sure that he would make good on that promise. He continued to prove himself over and over as a man whose word actually meant something. This cowboy was a keeper, and Callie had no doubts about that. Their bond was getting stronger by the day, and their partnership was about to be taken to the next level. Working alongside him on this mission might prove to be a challenge, but she was up for it.

After about 20 minutes in the Jacuzzi, Callie suggested a steak salad for dinner. Dom agreed, so they got out, dried off, changed clothes and went to the kitchen. The night air had cooled things off significantly, so Dom started a fire in the living room, and they ate by candlelight, sitting on the floor beside the coffee table. The steak salad really hit the spot and left enough room for dessert.

Callie got up to take the plates to the kitchen and Dom said, "Hey, I didn't stock up because I knew we were leaving. There's nothing sweet in there, but..."

"Don't worry, Cowboy. I've got you covered. Look what I brought," she said, pulling the brownies out of her purse.

"What? Have you been hiding those from me all day?"

"Some things are worth waiting for," she said, winking.

She went to the fridge to see if there was ice cream, but no luck. She did find a can of whipped cream in the fridge door, though, so she brought it over to the coffee table with the plates of brownies and set it down. Dom picked it up nearly as fast as she'd set it down, and squirted it right at Callie. Shocked at first, she took it from him and squirted it so that it landed right on his cheek. He got up to take the can back, but she began to run down the hallway, and the chase around the house was on.

Callie ended up back in the living room in front of the sofa, and Dom finally caught up to her, put his arms around her and they both fell onto the sofa. Dom took the can, but put it gently back onto the table and began to kiss the now runny cream off of Callie's nose. She returned the favor by kissing all the cream from his cheek. Dom whispered in her ear, "Even your delicious brownies can't hold a candle to you. You will always be the only dessert I will ever need."

Those words were the last ones necessary. The silence turned into more passionate kisses, and there by the light of the fire and candles, the brownies took second chair, waiting patiently as Callie and Dom shared their most favorite dessert. Then they ate the brownies, which seemed much more enjoyable. And after dinner, Callie and Dom returned to snuggle on the couch, falling asleep in each other's arms.

The morning light began to shine into the living room, and while neither Callie nor Dom wanted to move from their comfortable spot, it was time to wrap up a few more details. So with a quick breakfast of oatmeal and coffee, Callie left for home, and Dom finished up a few minor things on the ranch.

Sunday came and went as Callie tidied up the house, did what was left of the laundry, ran a few more errands and put her packed suitcase by the door. A full night's sleep without those pesky nightmares was a welcome surprise. She hadn't had them in several days, and she was hopeful that they were finally gone.

Dom arrived the next day around noon. Callie opened up her laptop and they sat next to each other on the patio and skyped Tom to let him know their expected arrival time. Tom thanked them again and told them he'd pick them up from the airport.

Afterwards, Callie started preparing for an early dinner while Dom sat down to map out the rest of the trip. The chicken was boiling, and the water for the mac and cheese was sitting in a pot on the stove, along with another pot with the potatoes in water. Callie had a few second thoughts on this meal prep because it always took so long, but she was determined to make it and there was plenty of time, so she decided to leave Dom to his planning and enjoy the process of what she knew would be the best meal she'd ever served her cowboy. The result had always been worth the time it took for grandma's favorite meal.

Dom could smell the stewing chicken and began to get hungry, so in an effort to help Callie, he went down to the country store and picked up tuna salad sandwiches and chips for the two of them to snack on. When he got back, they sat down to eat and went over the final details of the mission.

With the final plan in place, they relaxed for a while out on the patio with a cup of coffee and silence. It was time to put their game faces on. This was really important, and things could go wrong really fast, so it would take a team effort to pull off a successful mission and bring Emily home.

Dinner was finally ready at about 5:00, and just as Callie had surmised, Dom was grandma's newest fan. He ate every bite on his plate and got up for seconds and even thirds. She was watching him stuff down the last bite and started chuckling, saying, "You didn't like that very much, did you, Babe?"

Dom took a deep sigh and rubbed his stomach and then said, "That's the worst meal I've ever eaten three times in one sitting. Please don't make that again."

They both began to laugh, and sat for another 20 minutes, because they were both so full that they didn't want to think about moving. Because the dishes weren't going to march themselves to the dishwasher by themselves, they both agreed to share dish duty and retreat to the couch. Callie put a movie on, and they snuggled up while they watched a mindless comedy. It was a welcome distraction that allowed them to reset in preparation for the following day.

After the movie, both Callie and Dom were so physically and mentally drained that they went upstairs to bed. It was yet another early evening, but the alarm would be going off at 4:00 a.m., and a restful night's sleep was in order. Callie nestled into the crook of Dom's neck and fell asleep almost immediately.

The alarm went off, and Callie felt as if she'd just set it, but in her groggy state, she reached over to turn it off and realized that Dom wasn't there beside her. She called out for him and he said, "I'm downstairs, Darlin'. I wanted to get a jump on making breakfast for you before you got up."

Callie wasn't sure where this guy came from, but she was never letting him go. She told him she'd be down in a second and thanked him for always thinking of her, but she also thought to herself that he probably didn't get much sleep the night before. When she got downstairs, he'd made bacon and eggs and toast and had already loaded the truck up.

After getting their protein for the day and a shared shower and kisses, they poured two cups of coffee to go and headed off. Forty-five minutes later, they arrived at the airport. It was still dark out, but they could see the lights on the jet. It was fueled and ready for takeoff, and the pilot took their luggage as they boarded and belted in. Operation Reciprocity was in motion.

Chapter 3: Emotions in Check

San Juan, PR...

Tom awakened to the aroma of freshly brewed coffee. He hadn't slept very well through the night, and he knew it was because he was anxious about Dom and Callie's return to San Juan later in the day. He got up and put on a pair of jeans and a T-shirt, groggily walked to the kitchen to pour his first cup and took roast and vegetables out of the fridge to put in the crockpot for dinner. He wanted to host Callie and Dom with a hearty meal as a small way of saying thank you for their help in looking for Emily. As a special island treat, he would add fried plantains as an appetizer, with a garlic butter dipping sauce he'd come to enjoy. It was one of the few simple pleasures he'd found while living in Puerto Rico.

After stepping onto the deck to enjoy the ocean breeze while sipping his coffee, he picked up his iPad to read the digital version of the paper. Reading had become merely an exercise at this point, although he used to really enjoy it. Its only purpose now was to keep his mind occupied.

As he was struggling to get through the first few paragraphs of an article on life in the Florida Keys, he felt something land on his shoulder. He was just about to swat it away when he looked to his left and saw the most beautiful zebra longwing butterfly perched there, slowly fluttering its wings. It stayed on his shoulder, not moving. He reached to see if it would step over to his finger, and surprisingly, it did.

Gazing into its tiny eyes, he was reminded of an excursion he and Emily had made to a butterfly conservatory when she was 12. She had always loved butterflies. She'd said that they made her think of her mom, with their beauty and wings, and the walls in her room had been covered with beautiful butterfly cutouts she'd drawn and colored herself. On this particular trip, the conservatory housed several zebra butterflies, and Emily oohed and aahed over how beautiful and unique they were.

The memory of Emily's excitement over these little black-and-white beauties brought a smile to Tom's face, and the fact that one was sitting gingerly on his finger, still fluttering its wings at him, felt like a message of hope: that she was okay and she would be found. Tom was a doctor, and as such, had never quite been able to reconcile science with things like messages from the universe or God, but in his practice, he'd also seen many things that couldn't be explained, and it wasn't important to him to even try. He needed all the hope he could incorporate into his day, however it manifested itself.

Nearly as soon as he'd gotten used to the butterfly's tiny feet tickling his finger, it suddenly took flight. He watched it for as far as he could see it gracefully making its way into the clouds, and then he took another sip of coffee and smiled in comfort. He was at peace for the moment, and he was going to sit in silence with it, hanging on for as long as he could.

After an entire pot of coffee and a bagel with cream cheese for sustenance, it was time to prepare the crockpot for dinner, do a little dusting and light housekeeping for his guests, and finish packing for France. He'd gotten little details about the trip during his conversations with Dom and Callie, but Dom promised to discuss the specifics of the trip with him after they arrived.

Dom had sent a special visitor's badge issued by the FBI for Tom to be able to access the private strip at Friday Harbor Airport. It would take him about an hour to get to the airport, but he also wanted to stop at the Bacardi factory to purchase a special bottle of Bacardi Reserva Limitada for after-dinner drinks on the deck. That errand would take an extra hour, so there was just enough time to throw the ingredients in the crockpot, get things tidied up, grab a shower and leave.

The trip to the Bacardi factory was uneventful, making way for an easy drive to the airport. Traffic was light because it was nowhere near rush hour, so Tom was able to stop for an extra cup of coffee on his way. Just as he arrived at the airport, he got a text from Callie that they were about 30 minutes out. He pulled up to the chain-link gate of the private airstrip, and was greeted by a U.S. Customs agent, asking for ID. Flashing his badge, Tom couldn't help feeling a little like he was reenacting a scene from a Tommy Lee Jones movie when the agent motioned him forward and pointed to the private hangar parking area.

Tom sat in his car for what seemed like an eternity, checking his watch and then staring up at the sky, hoping for a glimpse of Callie and Dom's descent to the airport. Although he'd traveled to many parts of the world over the course of his medical career, including Alsace, none of those travels could ever compare to the one on which he was about to embark. He simply had to find Emily. There was no other result that he was willing to accept, and he was so grateful he didn't have to make the trip alone.

In almost exactly 25 minutes, the jet hit the runway, and never had Tom been so excited about the noise of screeching tires and engines reversing than he was this particular day. He got out of his car and made his way to the hangar just as the jet was pulling up to the blocks and turning off the engines. In just a few seconds, the door opened, the steps worked their way to the concrete, and his friends departed shortly thereafter, greeting Tom with warm hugs.

"Welcome back to Puerto Rico," Tom said. "You two certainly are a sight for sore eyes."

"It's so good to see you, Tom," Callie responded, smiling. "I certainly hope I look better than I did the last time you saw me."

Dom gave her a kiss on the cheek and said, "Darlin', that day was the day I got to take you home, so you never looked more beautiful to me than then."

"Aww, how sweet, Babe," said Callie.

Tom smiled at the two of them, thinking that it was nice to see how much they loved each other. After gathering up the luggage, they placed everything in the trunk of the car and headed back to Tom's to relax before dinner. The hour-long drive, however, prompted Tom to ask questions about the specifics of the plan, and Dom began to give him a briefing of what his sources had uncovered up to that point.

"Okay," Dom began. "So here's what we have so far. Now, I want to preface this by telling you not to get your hopes up. This is only our first lead, and may not pan out."

Tom said, "Okay. Whatever it is, it's better than I've come up with on my own. I just want to know what you have."

Continuing, Dom said, "The original field agent, Carrera, tracked down a possible sighting of Emily. Her photo had been uploaded and sent to INTERPOL, and using facial recognition, we identified that a young woman fitting Emily's description was photographed leaving Charles de Gaulle Airport in Paris with a group of young women. All of the young women were wearing head scarves and were being escorted out of the airport by several men and a woman fitting the description of Franco's wife, Ingrid.

Cameras throughout Paris tracked them as far out of the city as possible, but they were unable to get a tail on them before they left the city."

Callie was sitting quietly in the backseat, watching Tom's face as he heard the details. He seemed to be hanging on Dom's every word, and she was thinking about how difficult all of this had been on him.

Tom asked if that was the last known sighting, and Dom said, "Nothing on Emily since then, but using the same facial recognition technology, they were able to secure a match for one of the men in the group from a surveillance camera inside a bank in Strasbourg, France. That's where our search will begin, though."

It was about that time that Callie looked out the window and noticed they were passing by the private shuttle launch that she and Mercedes had gotten on to take their fateful trip to Franco and Ingrid's private island, and Callie was suddenly filled with anger. All the memories came rushing back of meeting Ingrid, thinking that she was so nice, to then being held captive by her and nearly drowning because of that wretched woman. The fact that Ingrid was still at large had haunted Callie since she'd left Puerto Rico.

"Callie? Did you hear me?" Tom asked.

Callie's attention quickly turned back to the conversation in the front seat, and she responded, "I'm sorry, I didn't. My mind was drifting. The flight must have taken more out of me than I thought. What did you say?"

Dom reached back and ran his fingers through Callie's hair, saying, "It's all right, Darlin'. We're going to take care of her together. She can run, but she can't hide."

Tom looked a little confused by Dom's comment, but Callie smiled and blew Dom a kiss, knowing that he could read her like a book he'd read many times over and could sense her fears. Just those few words calmed Callie's anger, and Tom asked his question again.

"Is pot roast okay for dinner? If not, I can make something else."

"I love pot roast, but really, anything is fine. You didn't have to go to all that trouble." Callie answered.

Tom laughed and said, "Trouble? You gave up your Texas lives to help me. That's trouble. Pot roast can't compare to that."

Dom, apparently feeling the need to add a little levity to the serious conversation they'd been having, said, "That really depends on the pot roast."

The three of them laughed, and the conversation turned to just how good the pot roast was going to be, and a few minutes later they were pulling into the driveway of Tom's beach house.

Dom got out and opened Callie's door, taking her hand to help her out of the car. That turned out to be a good thing, because her legs were a little wobbly from sitting for most of the day.

Tom grabbed the luggage and ushered them into the house. The aroma from the stewing meat and vegetables greeted them in an amazing Southern welcome, and Callie and Dom both commented on how they couldn't wait to taste it. Tom showed them to the very familiar guest room, where they freshened up while he got the oil ready for the plantains.

Callie came out to find Tom in the kitchen, smashing what looked like sliced bananas on a cutting board and asked, "What in the world are you doing, Tom? Getting out your aggression on bananas?"

Tom laughed heartily and said, "Sure. Wanna give it a try? It's great therapy."

Callie took the spatula from him and whacked one of the slices, completely flattening it so that now it looked like a pancake.

"That was fun!" Callie affirmed.

Dom walked into the kitchen and said, "What's all the excitement about?"

Callie showed him what she was doing, while Tom explained that they were similar to bananas, but that they were more savory than sweet and a favorite appetizer served at many of the local restaurants. He fried several and served them with the garlic sauce he'd made, and Dom and Callie told him how much they enjoyed them.

After the appetizers were gobbled up, dinner was ready, and the three of them sat down at the small kitchen table and began to get to know each other better. Dom wanted to find out as much about Emily as possible. It was crucial for him and Callie to get a better understanding of her personality, her favorite things, and any special memories she shared with her dad. Then he gave Tom details about his background in undercover work, and Callie shared how she had gone from falling in love with Dom to having to prove his innocence when he was arrested for murder, bringing her amateur sleuth skills to the attention of the feds.

Hearing Callie and Dom's personal story, Tom said, "Boy, you guys certainly don't do boring, do you? Your story would make for a fantastic movie."

Dom looked over at Callie and said, "Watching this beauty of mine every day is movie enough for me."

Tom smiled and said, "I understand why."

Callie blushed a little, smiled, and said, "You both should stop now. Otherwise, my head won't fit through the door when it's time to leave." Then she reached over, and with one hand on Dom's arm and one on Tom's, she added, "If it weren't for both of you, I wouldn't be here having this conversation. God's grace brought us to this table. Amen."

Simultaneously, Dom and Tom said, "Amen."

This seemed like the perfect opportunity to gather up the dinner dishes, and with the three of them working together, the kitchen was clean in 10 minutes. Shortly after, Tom served cocktails on the patio. The rum, combined with the warm tropical breeze and the sounds of the waves, proved to be a very relaxing end to the evening. It only took one glass for Callie to decide to call it a night, and Dom told her he'd be in shortly.

Once Callie had left the table, Dom took the opportunity to reassure Tom that he would do everything in his power to find Emily, but he also let him know how important it was to the investigation for Tom to have limited involvement.

As an example, Dom said, "You know how doctors aren't allowed to operate on family? Well, the same applies here, for the same reason. Our emotions get in the way of sound and reasonable judgment. The feds don't know you're with us, and I need to keep that as quiet as possible. Otherwise, they may pull the plug on the mission. I need your cooperation with that before we leave."

Tom said, "I understand. I'll stay in the background. You and Callie are in charge, and I'm grateful you're letting me come along. I won't do anything to jeopardize this mission. You have my word."

"Good deal. You see, that lady in there is my life, my partner. Having her here is both comforting and distracting. I'm fighting to keep my emotions in check about her participation. I can't handle another distraction, so knowing that I don't have another team member to worry about will help me keep my mind on the mission."

"As a surgeon, I understand the need to be free from distractions," Tom said. "You can count on me, Dom."

Getting up from the patio table, the two men finalized their mutual understanding with a handshake and a double tap on the back, agreeing that it was time to hit the hay. The next leg of the trip would be a long one, and a good night's rest was imperative.

Chapter 4: A Search for Truth

Somewhere in suburbia...

Emily had been restless during the last few weeks, trying to discover why she felt so displaced in her own life. She was becoming more and more frustrated that her memories wouldn't stay clearly focused, and Simon had begun to get increasingly controlling. Why could she not remember? Something about her circumstances just didn't feel right. She was almost completely hopeless and confined to this beautiful prison, but she had to find a way to remember.

Looking at the camera above while she was drinking the tea Simon had laid out for her, she opted not to finish it, picked up the current issue of *Natonal Geographic* and went to the garden room to read for a while. She thought that maybe something she read would spark a familiar piece of the puzzle. She was grasping at straws, she knew, but nothing was out of bounds at this point.

She sat down in the overstuffed, comfy chair next to the glass enclosure of the garden room and began flipping through the pages. She stopped when she saw a beautiful image of a very unusual butterfly. It was white, with black stripes, similar to a zebra, and its wings were longer than those of the butterflies she'd seen here.

Suddenly, from out of nowhere, a sense of something familiar came rushing in. She must have seen one of these before, but where and when were escaping her. Yes, she was sure of it, and the memory was becoming stronger. The same man she'd seen in her previous memory appeared once again in her mind's eye. He was holding her hand this time. They were walking down a concrete path and butterflies were everywhere, and one identical to the one in the magazine landed on her shoulder. This man had to be her dad. But what had happened to him? Had he died? Simon said he'd rescued her from the streets. Had she been homeless, or run away?

As the thoughts and questions raced through her mind, she immediately reminded herself that Simon was watching, so she quickly turned the page to find an article to read. He already seemed to be extra suspicious for some reason, and she didn't want to expose herself to even more control.

The night before had been their planned intimate night, and it had been less pleasant than usual. Emily was extremely grateful that she could rely on Simon's scheduled visits occurring only once per week. He wasn't abusive in a physical way, but he was very businesslike and unemotional in his approach to their weekly sex, but in their recent encounter, he'd gotten up abruptly and left the room without saying a word. This was certainly not any woman's dream of a romantic partner. He treated her as nothing more than a piece on his chessboard that he could easily put away when he was finished playing.

Emily's thoughts quickly went back to the zebra butterfly and the man she believed to be her dad. The memory was crystal clear now, and she wasn't going to let it go. The door would unlock in an hour, and she was going to find a bookstore at the mall. She didn't want to raise Simon's suspicions, so she couldn't risk flipping to that page in the magazine again, but the bookstore would certainly have the current edition, and Simon couldn't watch her there.

She picked up her purse and went to sit on the bench by the front door, and within about five minutes, the lock clicked open and she went to the car. Bonito ignored her morning greeting as usual, but Emily didn't care. She was on a mission to find another clue about her past, while the memory was still fresh in her mind.

As soon as the car stopped, Emily got out, waiting for Bonito to set the obligatory timer on her phone, and then she made her way to the mall directory to find the bookstore. Luckily, it was just around the corner and at the top of the escalator, so in less than a minute, she was inside. She couldn't afford to waste the precious time that she had available, so she asked the clerk to help her find the current issue of the magazine.

Opening the page to the article, she found it and stood at the magazine rack without concern for anyone around. Totally engrossed in the article, she discovered that these unique butterflies were indigenous to warmer climates. Not finding that to be extremely helpful to her goal, Emily flipped the page, and when she did, she saw a smaller photo of a conservatory. That was it! That was the place in her memory. She'd been there. She just knew it. The conservatory was in Key West, Florida.

Emily now had another piece of the puzzle, and she began to smile as if she'd just won some sort of grand prize. Would it lead to another clue? She wasn't sure, but it was at least a tiny piece of her past that she could hold onto. For the first time in nearly a year, her heart was full. The next piece of the puzzle had to come soon. It was almost unbearable to be completely in the dark about her past and have to rely on Simon to give her details.

After Emily left the bookstore, she decided she'd sit with a cup of coffee and a brownie. She loved chocolate, and today she was going to reward herself for calling up this lovely piece of the puzzle. She had no desire to buy anything else on this particular excursion to the mall. The only thing that really mattered was maintaining the memories she'd uncovered and recalling more of them.

While enjoying every delectable bite of her double chocolate brownie and peppermint mocha coffee, the image of the handsome man holding her hand brought yet another smile. She had to search for the truth. She began to think about her life with Simon and how difficult it was going to be to do that. His truth was all that she'd known, but with all the locked doors and cameras and the isolated nature of their home life, was his truth fact or some strange fiction? And if he'd been lying to her, was her father out there somewhere, wondering where she was?

Alsace, France

The small jet pulled into the tiny hangar on yet another private airstrip at the Baset-Mulhouse Airport in Northern Alsace. The team exited the plane and took their luggage over to the car that was waiting for them, courtesy of their French connection, Gabrielle. They would make contact with her after settling in at the little bed and breakfast located on one of the local vineyard properties in the Upper Rhine Valley.

Driving through, Callie thought that the beautiful Alsace wine region was one of the most spectacular landscapes she had ever seen. Even though it was still very cold this time of year, the beauty of the ice-capped mountains in the distance was captivating. Tom remarked at how much difference 15 hours of flight time could make in both the view and the climate, and both Dom and Callie agreed. They'd gone from white sandy beaches and 80 degrees at midday to snowflakes and mountains.

The bed and breakfast was far enough out of the way that the team could fit in perfectly as American tourists, but close enough to be able to get to Bergheim, where Gabrielle had spotted Ingrid in a little café, Bistrot du Chevaliers. The fact that they were staying in one of the most beautiful areas of France, in a region that claimed worldwide fame for its Rieslings, was just the icing on the chocolate cake for Callie.

Dom, having finished unpacking before Callie, asked, "Hey, Darlin', how about I start a pot of coffee?"

"Oh, you read my mind, Babe. I'll step across the hall and see if Tom wants to join us," Callie replied. "I'll be right back."

Tom was just closing the closet door when Callie walked in and told him he had to try a fresh cup of French brew, and he was in the process of walking over when a strikingly beautiful brunette appeared in the hallway. He stopped to take in as much of her as he could as she continued to walk his way with a very charming smile. She was dressed in a matte royal blue leather suit, with a black-and-white floral silk blouse, and legs that could knock a man's eyes out.

She smiled, walking right up next to him, and extended her hand. Tom was so awestruck that he couldn't manage a single word, but Dom and Callie, noticing Tom's awkward appearance, walked to the doorway to see what was going on.

"Bonjour, Gabrielle!" Dom said, smiling. "It's great to see you again! Let me introduce you to Tom, since he's clearly at a loss for words. I see you still know how to command a room."

Tom's face turned a slightly pale shade of pink, but attempting to pick up the fumble, he extended his hand to greet her and said, "When beauty walks into your life, you don't want to blow it with words. You just embrace the favor from the gods."

Callie said, "Tom, are you a closet cowboy? That was a really good save."

Dom's eyebrows rose as if he'd just been one-upped and said, "I'm stealing that one, my man. You just put me to shame."

Tom added, "Well, you can have this one, because you did give me time to pull it out of my hat."

Gabrielle said, "Bonjour, Dominic! I see you still know how to embarrass a room. Enchantée, Tom. It's so nice to meet you. What a lovely compliment. Thank you very much."

Dom then introduced Gabrielle to Callie, saying, "Gabrielle, this is Special Agent Callie Fletcher, my partner, in every sense of the word," placing his arm around her shoulder. The two women smiled and shook hands, and all four of them went into the room, closing the door behind them, and talked over coffee.

Gabrielle began the conversation by updating everyone on what had transpired over the past week. She'd seen Ingrid entering Bistrot du Chevalier on a fairly regular basis. Gabrielle had befriended one of the female bartenders there, which made it much easier to gain access to Ingrid's comings and goings without calling attention to herself. She'd learned that Ingrid had been using the restaurant as the home base for making contact with wealthy businessmen who were interested in purchasing her human commodities.

The barmaid had turned out to be an excellent source of information, because Ingrid was rude to her every time she'd come in for drinks. Gabrielle had used this as an advantage and commiserated with the barmaid, because she knew that women had no problem talking about one another when they felt they had a comrade. Through her conversations with the young barmaid, Gabrielle had been able to discover that Ingrid was making backdoor deals with these men, selling them a commodity she referred to as "lovebirds" and that these so-called lovebirds were selling to the tune of six hundred thousand American dollars apiece.

Gabrielle had further learned that about a year before, Ingrid had met with a very handsome, gray-haired gentleman from the States. The barmaid had overheard them talking about his interest in purchasing one of these lovebirds, and Ingrid agreed to show him her collection after a deposit of 25 percent had been made to her numbered bank account in the Caymans.

This conversation over very expensive birds had heightened the barmaid's suspicions, and that's when she began to pay special attention to this arrogant woman's dealings and table conversation with all of the different men she met with at the café. She'd made it her mission to serve Ingrid's table, no matter how rude she was, because she just knew there was something very sinister going on.

Dom and Callie's eyes lit up as Gabrielle enlightened them on everything she'd learned just in the last week from her new, very talkative confidante. It was as if they'd been handed the golden egg without having to purchase the goose.

"Wow!" Dom said. "We need to recruit this barmaid. She's done most of the legwork for us. Did she, by any chance, hear where Ingrid was living?"

"No, but that should be easy enough to find out. She makes reservations before she comes, to be sure she gets the same table every time, and she has one on the book for tomorrow at 3:00 in the afternoon," Gabrielle responded.

The timing couldn't have been more perfect, and the parts of the clock fit together perfectly to signal the chime of the first bell. The one concerning factor was that Ingrid had already seen Dom and Callie's faces, so they couldn't risk being seen by her. In the process of formulating a plan, Gabrielle suggested that she and Tom head into town. Tom could pose as Gabrielle's American boyfriend, and they could strategically locate themselves at the coffee shop across the street from the bistro about an hour before Ingrid was scheduled to arrive. Once Ingrid went inside, Tom could be the lookout while Gabrielle quickly placed a tiny magnetic tracker under the wheel well of Ingrid's car.

Callie said, "We're concerned about Tom being too closely involved. Dom and I talked about this with Tom, but just so you know, Tom's daughter is the one we're looking for. I'm not sure if Dom had the opportunity to talk to you about that, Gabrielle."

Dom nodded in agreement with Callie, adding, "Yeah, things were put together so quickly, Gabrielle, that I'm not sure we talked about Tom even being with us on this trip. We agreed to let him come, but his emotional tie to the case and his lack of field training could be problematic."

Tom had been sitting quietly, listening to the conversation, but at this point, he interrupted before Gabrielle could respond. "Uh, Tom's in the room, people. I'm a grown man, and I'm the one who has the most to lose and the most to gain here. So it seems to me that I should have some part in the discussion about what my role should or shouldn't be."

Tom's comments gave way to complete silence, and Dom said, "You have the floor and our complete attention, sir. My most sincere apologies for forgetting what's truly at stake for you."

"Thank you, Dom. I'm well aware of the risks here, and there's no way I want to jeopardize any plan to find my daughter. Even though I'm not a trained FBI field agent, I am a trained surgeon, and like any operation, the perfect plan of attack oftentimes changes once the plan is set in motion. That seems to be what we're dealing with here. The bottom line is, Gabrielle needs an extra set of eyes, and mine are perfectly capable. Since I'm not actually doing anything except sitting, watching and enjoying this beautiful woman's company, aside from the risk of perhaps making a fool of myself again, I don't see the issue."

Gabrielle smiled politely at Tom and waited for a response from Dom and Callie.

"All right," Dom agreed. "But we need to be sure that if something goes wrong, you're not going to get involved. In that case, Callie and I will be in a nearby discreet location, in the car. We're going to give you one of our watches that's all set to transmit audio. That way, we'll know what's going on without being seen, but we'll be close enough to take action if we have to."

Everyone agreed that this was the best strategy to take, and that the risk was as minimal as possible to Tom, given the circumstances. Once the tracking device was in place, the satellite tracking system would lead them right to her front door, where they would hopefully find Emily.

"Operation Catch and Release" was now a go, and Gabrielle excused herself to get ready for the following day, leaving the rest of the crew to relax and unwind after their 15-hour flight. Tom went back to his room to attempt to take a short nap, and Dom and Callie decided to take a walk around the property. They agreed to meet downstairs for dinner, which would be served promptly at 7:00.

From the front porch of the beautiful B&B, Callie looked off in the distance and could see the Vosges mountains. The fog had lifted with the afternoon sun, and it had turned out to be a beautiful day. Dom took her hand and they walked down the front porch steps and around the corner to the entry of the vineyards. Callie relished in the warmth of his hand, walking along the paths of the vines that would soon be filled with grapes and imagining her return with him one day, to immerse herself in her heritage.

Callie paused for a second to snap a shot of what she surmised had to be the Grand Ballon, the highest peak of the Vosges. The sun had begun to descend somewhere behind the peak, and as she turned to show Dom the photo, he said, "Still doesn't compare to the view standing before me, Darlin'."

She got up on her tiptoes and gave him a passionate, lingering kiss. Dom had to catch his breath from the kiss, and

Callie took the opportunity to say, "A French kiss in France. It was imperative that we do that."

Dom said, "You know, they say if you do something seven times, it becomes a habit. Let's test that theory."

Callie giggled, and then wholeheartedly agreed, even though kissing her cowboy was a habit she'd already grown accustomed to. Any opportunity to reinforce this particular habit was a welcome opportunity, and things were about to get very serious, so she was taking full advantage of the simple pleasures.

After only about 30 minutes of walking, the temperature began to decline, and Dom suggested they head back to the room to shower, change and snuggle for a while before meeting Tom for dinner. Callie's nervous energy seemed to have disappeared at this point, so a shower and a snuggle with her cowboy sounded like heaven.

As Callie opened the front door of the B&B, she and Dom were greeted with the aroma of sauerkraut from the kitchen. Dinner was definitely being prepared, and at least one of the items on the menu was apparent. As they moved up the stairs, the aroma followed, and Dom mentioned to Callie that he was going to have a hard time relaxing because the aroma was making him hungry.

"Don't worry, Cowboy. I brought reinforcements from home. We can snack in bed before dinner."

Dom unlocked the door to their room and said, "I think I like this new partnership thing, Darlin'."

Callie quickly replied, "Well, that's a good thing, because I'm not going anywhere."

After a refreshing shared shower and a change of clothes, Callie set up a tray of chips, pepper jack cheese and salsa, and placed it in the center of the bed. Then they snuggled up together on one side of the tray and began to nibble on their mini Texas treats while talking about their strategy for the days to come.

An hour later, it was time to join Tom for dinner downstairs, so they put the snacks in the tiny room fridge, put on their shoes, and found him waiting for them in the hallway. When Callie saw the food laid out buffet style alongside the table in the dining room, her eyes lit up. It looked like a combination French-German restaurant, with offerings of lobster soufflé, sauerkraut with sausage and potatoes, and a sampling of white cheeses, fruits and breads.

Bottles of white wine and dark beer were sitting next to each other, as well as bottles of Perrier; both were a popular choice for meals in Alsace. Callie opted for a glass of chardonnay, because she was anxious to try the lobster. The men went straight for the beer and sauerkraut.

They sat down with their plates, and Tom closed his eyes to say grace over the meal. Dom and Callie followed suit. With just the three of them at the dinner table, it was a quiet few minutes of silent prayer, followed by a simultaneous amen and digging in to their scrumptious first meal together on foreign soil. The dessert cart was brought 20 minutes later, offering warm crepes, an assortment of French pastries, vanilla poached plums, and petit fours.

Dom's sweet tooth kicked in, and he sampled one of each. Callie resisted the temptation and chose the plums, and Tom decided he'd take an éclair for later. Each of them took a small pour of pinot noir with dessert, and when they were completely stuffed, they agreed to retire to their respective rooms for the night.

The bed was extremely comfortable and sufficiently warm, and Callie practically melted into the luxurious sheets as soon as she felt them touch her body. Dom was lying next to her, but sensed that Tom might need a little shoring up, so after Callie got settled into a sound sleep, he got up and went across the hall.

Tapping lightly on the door, Tom answered. He invited Dom in and told him that he hadn't even attempted to sleep because he knew his efforts would be futile. He was just too wired to sleep. Dom sat and talked with him for the next few hours, letting him share more of his story. The one thing that Dom had learned in his undercover work was that allowing someone to tell their story seemed to help them relieve their anxiety. He'd become an artful listener.

This time was no different than all the other experiences he'd had with people. He could see that Tom's eyes were glossy and he was waning as his mind relaxed and allowed his body to take over. Taking his cue, Dom got up, reassured Tom that things were taking a positive turn now, told him to get some sleep, and went back across the hall to join Callie and do the same.

The alarm went off at 8:00 a.m., and Callie hit the buzzer, told Dom to stay in bed, and she went downstairs to bring a breakfast tray of goodies up for him and Tom. She loaded up the tray with a variety of croissants, jam, cheese, ham, orange juice and coffee and traversed the stairs, lightly kicking Tom's door with her foot.

He took the tray from her and helped himself to a croissant and coffee. Dom must have heard her, because he joined them in Tom's room for breakfast. Gabrielle had called while Callie was downstairs, and Dom had asked her to join them for breakfast. She appeared in the doorway just as they were finishing their first cup of coffee.

Tom's smile reappeared when he saw Gabrielle standing there, and he bid her good morning and walked across the hall to get a chair for her while Callie poured her a cup of coffee. The four of them enjoyed a leisurely breakfast together and decided to leave earlier than originally planned to get in a bit of sightseeing before planting themselves at their surveillance posts.

Callie and Dom gave Tom the special watch they'd told him about, and showed him how to turn it on. They would be in separate vehicles, and so they would need to test it to be sure they had clear communication at a range safe enough to be out of sight. They went over the plan again, and when everyone was clear about the precise details, Callie and Dom went back to their room to secure everything they'd need for the trip.

Tom and Gabrielle left in her vehicle for Bergheim, but took a side trip along the wine route so that Gabrielle could show Tom a private lake she'd found. The views were spectacular, and she wanted him to see it. They parked the vehicle and got out to walk through a little grove of trees, and in the clearing, a beautiful lake appeared. There were a bevy of swans attempting to land, but the lake was still slightly frozen, so they flew on.

The two sat on the rocks beside the lake and began to talk. There was something about Gabrielle that made Tom feel safe, and he began to tear up as he shared how desperate he was to find Emily. She reached over to wipe the teardrops that were now trickling down, and then she kissed him softly on the cheek.

Without missing a step, he took her in his arms and kissed her passionately. Taken aback and swept away by the emotion, she kissed him back. Once Gabrielle came up for breath, she told him that it probably wasn't wise to go further but gave him a reassuring peck on the cheek, and they went back to the car to proceed on their journey into Bergheim.

About a minute later, Tom heard Dom's voice say, "Just letting you guys know that the watch works."

Laughter ensued in both vehicles, and 45 minutes later, Bergheim came into view. Gabrielle pointed out that the masonry walls surrounding Bergheim were built in the 14th century, and they were still standing. She also made note that in the 16th and 17th centuries, Bergheim held several witch trials, sending 40 women to their death for sorcery.

Callie and Dom had been following behind several kilometers, but took a turn which led them onto a side street instead of going through the center of the village. They found an inconspicuous location on the street in front of a pharmacy, put on their disguises and walked across the street for a quick cup of coffee and a tour of the synagogue.

Tom and Gabrielle parked in front of the café across from Bistrot du Chevalier and walked around town for several hours, looking in shop windows and being touristy. At about 2:00, they walked back to the café and went inside to get a table next to the front window. Once seated, Tom took out a map and several brochures so that it would appear that they were planning their trip through the countryside. The waitress appeared at the table to take their order, and even though they weren't hungry, they ordered a plate of bread and cheese with coffee. This would allow them to sit for as long as they wanted and wait for Ingrid to show up.

Gabrielle and Tom spent the hour or so talking about the history of Bergheim and the surrounding cities, nibbling on their plate of food. At precisely 2:55, a black Land Rover drove up and Ingrid emerged from it, heading into the bistro. Gabrielle gave Callie and Dom the signal that she'd arrived by saying, "Oh, look at the lovely birdcage in the shop across the street. I'm going to go over and snap a shot of it for our photo album. I'll be right back."

She waited for a few minutes and then got up from the table, walked across and took her camera out of her purse, along with the magnetic tracking device. Tom watched as she walked past the Land Rover and, as if she'd done it a million times, in one slick motion, she was past the Land Rover, snapping random photos, and then quickly back to the table with Tom.

Once she returned to the table, she gave her final signal to Dom that the task was complete, saying, "This one's definitely for the books," at which point Dom and Callie started back to the bed and breakfast to monitor her from there. Gabrielle and Tom met back up with them an hour later, which was about the same time that Ingrid's vehicle began to move.

The red dot on the screen moved from Bergheim and traveled up the winding roads into the mountains, where it finally stopped. Callie had been timing the track, and it appeared to be about an hour's drive northeast from Bergheim, which would make it about the same distance from their location.

Once they were certain that the vehicle had reached its final destination, they accessed the FBI's satellite feed, which provided them with live realtime images. The Land Rover was parked in front of a castle, but it was joined by several other black Land Rovers. There were clearly a number of people inside, but how many, and who were they?

Dom clicked a button to turn on the infrared cameras on the satellite software, citing that a major advantage of working with an intelligence agency was the technology it had available. Seeing through walls had become the norm in the spy world long before the public at large knew of its existence. The cameras quickly booted up and Callie and Dom began to count the red images on the screen.

In an area on the right-hand side of the castle, there appeared to be approximately 20 people. At the opposite end and to the rear, on the cliff side of the castle, there were ten additional people with three more just to the exterior. Dom thought that the 10 huddled together on the left might be the captive women, and that the rest of the people in the castle were likely guards.

After collaborating for a few minutes about what this new recon uncovered, Callie, Dom and Gabrielle knew it was time to call in reinforcements. Dom knew just the team for the job. He quickly picked up his phone and placed a call to his old friend, Jim Spade, an ex-Navy SEAL, whose team he'd worked with on his last mission in Turkey. These guys could get in and secure a fortress quicker than any team he'd ever seen, and their expertise was certainly required here.

Jim answered immediately and agreed to help. Dom sent him all the intel they had gathered up to that point, and Jim said that his team was nearby and that he'd get back with him in a few hours with a plan of action. Because of the location of the castle, it would present certain challenges, but Jim assured Dom that they could overcome them.

Dom hung up the phone and updated the others on the call. While Callie and Gabrielle seemed to be hanging on his every word, Dom noticed that Tom was staring at the computer images on the screen. He stopped in midsentence, drawing the ladies' attention over to Tom.

Callie said, "Tom, are you okay?"

"Sure," he said. "I just can't take my eyes off the screen. One of those people could be my Emily, and this is the closest I've felt to her since she left for Puerto Rico."

Gabrielle placed her hand on Tom's and said, "You're going to have her back soon, Tom. I'm sure of it."

Callie suggested they have a glass of wine while they were waiting for news from Jim. Everyone else agreed, and the four of them went downstairs to get a late afternoon snack and wine. Dom took Callie aside on the way down and whispered in her ear, "Keep a close eye on him, Darlin'. Things may get hairy in the next 24 hours." Callie gave a silent nod, assuring him that she would.

After a torturous few hours of playing the waiting game, Dom's phone rang and he put Jim on speakerphone as he went over the details of the tactical plan. As it happened, the entire team was just finishing up a job in Germany, just across the border from Alsace, and they would be ready to go at midnight.

They'd fly in via helicopter, landing at a ski lodge helipad on the slope adjacent and a few hundred feet above the castle's location. They'd then hang glide in, approaching the castle from its uppermost floor on the side near what they believed was the room where the women were located. Once they had the guards quietly taken out on the second floor, the first floor could then be secured. At that point, Dom and his team would be free to enter the castle and ascertain if Emily was there.

Callie was mesmerized by the sheer miracle of pulling this off so quickly. These guys were dead-on professionals, and she was clearly out of her league when it came to the spy world. She was just happy to be along for the ride, and this was going to be a wild one.

Dom hung up the phone after greenlighting the mission, and Callie and Gabrielle began preparing for their trek up the mountainside. It would be dark and perhaps treacherous to drive the winding roads that led up to the castle, and because they didn't know the terrain, they'd need to leave earlier than necessary and find a stopping point nearby to wait for the all clear from Jim.

In the middle of all the flurry of activity, Tom had stepped over to his room, and Callie noticed he was sitting on the bed, staring out the window. She walked over, sat down beside him and put her hand on his shoulder. She knew his mind must be racing with thoughts of every possible scenario, and wanting to comfort him, she said, "You know, when Dom was arrested for murder and I was unsure about the outcome of those dire circumstances, I did something that really helped me."

Tom looked at her and asked, "What was that, Callie?"

Callie pointed towards the night sky and said, "I looked to the stars. You see those two stars up there? They always seem to be watching over me. I like to imagine them as my daddy and my late husband, Mike, because it makes me feel better to know they're there. Find a star, my friend. I feel like Emily's mom is up there somewhere, watching over her. Don't you?"

Tom smiled at her, looked up and pointed to a bright, twinkling star sitting next to the ones she'd pointed out to him. Looking back at her, he said, "You know, you're right. Just imaging that's her, shining her beauty down on me, makes me feel better. Thank you, Callie. I needed something to hang onto."

"Don't we all, my friend. You hang onto that thought. We're almost there."

Callie patted him on the arm and walked back into the room where Dom and Gabrielle were nearly finished preparing. Dom, realizing how difficult staying behind would be for Tom, suggested that since the majority of the heavy lifting would be done by Jim and his team, it would be acceptable for Tom to come along with them to the castle. Tom was relieved and thanked all three of them for what they were doing to help him, and at approximately 10:00 p.m., they went down to the car and began their trip up the mountain.

The roads were less difficult to navigate than Gabrielle had imagined, though there were a few slippery spots along the way. Dom drove, and Callie was extremely happy about that because he knew his way around a tricky road better than anyone she'd ever met. It took nearly an hour and a half, but they reached a lookout point about four kilometers from the castle where there was room to pull off the road and park, and they sat in the quiet, waiting.

At midnight, Dom got the signal from the comlink that he'd set up with Jim. They'd landed on the helipad and were prepping to glide. At 12:10, the next signal came. All systems go. Descending on the castle. Nothing came across for the next 20 minutes, but just as the team was beginning to express concern, the final signal came at 12:34. The all clear was given.

Dom cranked up the car, and five minutes later, Dom, Callie, Gabrielle and Tom drove up to the castle and parked at the front door. And what a magnificent door it was. Callie said, "I don't believe I've ever seen, or for that matter, even imagined, a red door on a castle. But I suppose this is France, so..."

Dom looked over at her and said, "The French believe that painting a door red brings good fortune to its inhabitants."

"Really?" Callie asked.

"No. I just made that up, but it sounded good, didn't it?"

Tom piped in and said, "Okay. I know what you guys are doing, but it's not working. When can we go in?"

Tom had seen right through Dom and Callie's attempt to distract him for a little while longer before they entered, so Dom explained that he wanted to wait until Jim opened the front door; that sometimes an all clear can turn into something slightly less than that.

Tom understood, and waited, however impatiently. But 30 seconds later, the front door swung open, and Ingrid came running out. Everyone jumped out of the car to stop her, but Callie was faster than the rest and got to her first. Ingrid was unarmed this time, and Callie's Southern blood began to boil when she saw her face. All of the memories of Puerto Rico came rushing back in a split second, and Callie rushed Ingrid, knocking her to the ground.

Dom came up behind Callie, but as she heard him nearing and yelling her name, she said, "Step back, Cowboy. She's all mine."

Ingrid, now flat on her back on the cold, hard concrete driveway, with Callie sitting on top of her, looked up at Callie and said, "Take your best shot, little girl."

That was all it took for Callie to punch Ingrid smack in the mouth, saying, "That was for my cowboy."

"Is that all you've got?" Ingrid asked, spitting out the blood from her mouth.

"In Texas, we serve the appetizer first. Here's the main course," completely coldcocking her into a semiconscious state. "That one was for me," Callie added as she got to her feet and stepped backwards, shaking her now-throbbing hand.

"Darlin', remind me never to throw you overboard," Dom said, with a look of astonishment on his face.

Gabrielle and Tom stood next to each other, smiling at what they'd just observed. And within seconds, Jim was standing in the doorway of the castle, giving his final clearance and then raising his eyebrows at a bloody Ingrid on the ground.

One of Jim's team cuffed Ingrid, got her to her feet and took her back inside, and Tom quickly went into the living room where all the girls had been gathered by the team. He looked through the group of ten, but the tears began to stream down his face as he realized Emily was not among them.

He angrily lunged for Ingrid, but Dom stopped him, warning him that it wouldn't help them find Emily. The team began to ask questions of the young women about any knowledge they had of Emily's whereabouts, but this group had only been there for a month and had never seen her.

Jim and his team began to search the castle for any evidence that might give them further leads. While they were doing that, Dom noticed Callie's hand had begun to swell, so he went into the kitchen to get some ice out of the freezer for her. Reaching into the freezer, he took out the ice bin, and as he began to scoop up the ice, he noticed something black down at the bottom of the bin. He dumped the ice in the sink, and a black book inside a triple coating of cellophane and tucked into a plastic baggie fell into the sink on top of the ice.

He picked up the book and called Callie into the kitchen. He didn't want to alert Tom just yet, so he and Callie quietly opened the book to see what was inside. They'd hit pay dirt. Ingrid had kept a ledger of every dirty detail of her human trafficking activities, dating back ten years.

They thumbed through the pages around the time of Emily's disappearance, and there it was. They called Tom and Gabrielle into the kitchen, and handed Tom the book with the page open to the pertinent information.

Tom read the details out loud while Dom took care of Callie's hands. Emily was purchased by a man named Simon Baker. A tiny headshot of his photo was glued next to a similar headshot of Emily. Tom was devastated that his daughter had been sold as if she were a piece of chattel, a trinket. At the same time, this was the first solid piece of evidence that she was alive, at least as of 15 months before.

Dom asked Gabrielle to do a quick scan of this man's photo to see what it turned up, and within the course of about 45 seconds, a driver's license record appeared. Simon was living in a city by the name of Murfreesboro, Tennessee. It was clear where they were headed next. They hadn't found Emily here, but they had just busted one of the largest, longest running human trafficking rings in history. Ingrid would spend the rest of her life in prison, and with the discovery of her book, the hope was that hundreds of women could be returned to their families.

INTERPOL was called in to take custody of Ingrid and the group and get the young women to the local hospital to be checked out and ultimately back home. Callie, Dom, Tom and Gabrielle went back to the B&B to get packed up and on their way to Tennessee. Gabrielle's part of the mission would end here, but she and Tom agreed to stay in touch. She said her good-byes and wished them good fortune in the next phase of the mission.

Dom placed a call to Agent Carrera with a status update, as promised, and the jet was ready by the time they got to the hangar. No one would ever have guessed that Emily would be stateside, much less a tiny southern state right in the middle of the Bible belt. She had been closer to home than Tom knew. It was mind boggling, but they were grateful for the lead and one step closer to a father-daughter reunion.

Chapter 5: Music City Roundup

Private Airport, Smyrna, TN...

The jet taxied down the short runway distance and turned the corner towards its destination, Hangar 13. Callie was experiencing the effects of jetlag. Due to the fatigue and the multiple time zones her body had been through over the last few days, she realized she had no idea what day of the week it was. She reached for her cell phone to confirm the day and time, and saw that it was Tuesday, 9:45 a.m.

Dom's phone rang just before the jet came to a final stop, and he picked it up to see that it was Agent Carrera with an update for him. Carrera had made contact with the Nashville FBI field office immediately after Dom's call from the Alsatian castle. The Nashville agents had immediately set up surveillance of the last known address listed on Simon's Tennessee driver's license and had already confirmed that it was his current residence. The property was a large, gated estate located just outside Murfreesboro, Tennessee, a suburb of Nashville.

Carrera had just received word that Emily had been spotted getting into the backseat of a limo. A tail was initiated, and the limo stopped, dropped Emily off and parked just a few feet away from the entrance of a large mall in Franklin, another suburb of Nashville 30 minutes west of the Smyrna Airport where the team had just landed.

Callie had done a little of her own reconnaissance on the long flight back to the States. Simon had no adult criminal record, he had made a fortune in the internet security business, he paid his taxes, and appeared to be an upstanding American citizen. With a little further digging into his history, however, Callie discovered that Simon had been arrested at 17 on a misdemeanor stalking charge in his hometown of Boise, Idaho.

The victim was a 15-year-old girl, and a no-contact order had been issued, but the charges had been dropped and the records were ordered sealed. Fortunately for them, their investigation of human trafficking on an international scale had allowed access to those sealed records.

Dom and Callie now had somewhat of a partial picture of who Simon was and the significant control he may have over Emily. He was an expert in his field, and with his history of stalking, he most definitely would be tracking her every move. Though they were curious as to why he might allow her to venture out on her own outside the estate, it didn't really matter because it presented them with the perfect opportunity to rescue her.

Dom and Callie had to hit the ground running. There was no time to waste. Tom insisted on going with them, and Dom thought it might be a good idea, given that Emily may need to see a familiar face, but Tom was instructed to stand just inside the entrance to the mall where Emily had been dropped. Locating her would be a challenge in a mall full of people, but the limo's location seemed the most logical place to station themselves.

The team quickly gathered their gear and got into the Mercedes SUV that was waiting for them. They were in Franklin in under 30 minutes, and they were grateful that traffic was much lighter than it was in the Austin area. Once they were on the road circling the mall's perimeter, they made contact with the local FBI agents who were still surveilling the limo.

Several plain-clothed agents were already inside, attempting to locate Emily, but they had been unsuccessful. Dom, Callie and Tom quickly exited the SUV and went into the mall's main entrance near the food court on the second level. Tom sat on a bench just inside the entrance so that he could watch every single patron's exit.

Callie and Dom headed to the escalator, but as they approached it together, Dom said, "Darlin', I think we can cover more ground if we split up, don't you?"

"Absolutely," Callie responded. "You go downstairs. I'll look in some of the smaller shops first and keep you updated, Babe."

Callie knew one thing about herself and hoped that Emily was the same. She detested large department stores in the mall because she was overwhelmed by the merchandise and found it hard to make shopping decisions. The smaller stores were easier to navigate, and she could also tell by looking across the entirety of the merchandise whether she'd even bother going inside. The small store layout would also allow her to spot Emily quickly.

With that thought in mind, she went to the bath and body products store first. She could easily see that Emily wasn't there and stepped across the way to the bookstore that she'd spotted. There were too many people inside to get a great view from the outside, so she moved through the aisles at a much faster pace than she'd ever thought possible, but Emily wasn't there either.

Coming out of the bookstore, she noticed a small tea shop in the corner adjacent to one of the department stores. Walking closer, she got a glimpse of the back of a young woman who fit Emily's body style. She walked inside to get a good look at her face, and there she stood.

Callie whispered into her watch, "Subject located. Tea store, upper level, southwest corner beside Dillard's."

Dom confirmed notification, but knew he would have to reiterate his instructions to Tom and said, "Tom, sit still. We don't know what we're dealing with yet. We'll bring her to you."

Emily had her nose down to a tin of tea as Callie walked up next to her and struck up a conversation. She quietly and calmly said, "Emily, don't look up, and don't be afraid. You don't know me, but my name is Special Agent Callie Fletcher. I'm with the FBI, and I've been working with your father to find you."

Emily's initial reaction was shock and disbelief. She followed Callie's instructions at first, but then she began to think that this may be another one of Simon's tricks, to test her loyalty, and she knew the punishment that would be coming her way. Besides, she wasn't even sure if her father was alive. She decided she wasn't willing to risk the consequences, and as a kneejerk reaction, she threw the tea tin at Callie and began to run out of the store through the food court.

"Subject in the wind. Moving towards the food court exit," Callie said into her watch as she breathlessly chased after Emily. People were beginning to stare, and Callie knew things were about to get dicey. Dom met Callie as she rounded the corner into the food court, where people and tables and chairs were interfering with their line of sight.

When they finally made their way through the crowd of onlookers, Tom and Emily were standing face to face, silent and completely motionless, staring at one another. Dom and Callie listened as Tom began to talk softly to Emily without making an advance toward her. He began to recount a trip down memory lane for Emily, and although she wasn't walking away, she didn't appear to be convinced by anything he'd said... until he began to sing.

"You're the end of the rainbow, my pot of gold. You're Daddy's little girl, to have and to hold. A precious gem..."

Tom's voice was now quivering, and Emily took a step towards him and said, "Daddy?"

"Yes, Baby Girl. It's me," Tom said, and the tears of joy began to flow as he grabbed Emily tightly to embrace her.

Callie's tears had already covered her cheeks by that time, and as she looked over at Dom, he was wiping his eyes as well. The crowd began to clap, even though Callie wasn't sure if they knew exactly what they were clapping for.

In the midst of all the noise and excitement, the alarm on Emily's stopwatch went off, and she suddenly realized that Bonito would be on his way and that Simon wouldn't be very far behind. She looked up at Tom, not fully remembering everything about him but knowing for certain he was her dad, and said, "He's coming to get me. He won't let me go."

Tom looked deep into her eyes and said, "He's never dealt with me and my rowdy Texas friends, Dom and Callie."

Emily looked back over at Callie and smiled, and Dom said, "He's right, Emily. Simon isn't in charge now. You are. We have a jet waiting to take you home. What do you say we show Simon who's really the boss here?"

Emily said, "I'm in."

The crowd parted, allowing the four of them access to the exit, but Bonito was walking inside at the same time. He rushed toward Emily to grab her, but Tom laid him flat on his back with the full force of a single punch, energized by more than a year's worth of anger, frustration and sadness.

Tom took Emily by the hand and hurried outside, followed by Dom and Callie. It was finally time to go home. Dom alerted the new pilot to fire up the jet and be ready to fly in the next half hour. Tom got into the backseat of the SUV and held Emily the entire way back to the Smyrna Airport.

Dom and Callie were holding hands in the front seat, allowing a father and his daughter to reunite with as much privacy as could be afforded in a vehicle. The car was back at the hangar in record time, and the jet's engines were already going when they got out of the car.

They boarded the jet and waited for the pilot to announce their departure, but after a few minutes, when nothing was happening, Dom went up front to see what the delay was. He opened the cockpit to a gun-brandishing wild-eyed Simon. The pilot and copilot were bound and gagged in the corner.

Simon backed Dom out of the cockpit and into the galley, where they were both now in full view of Callie, Tom and Emily. Emily whispered, "See, Daddy! I told you he wouldn't let me go. He's always watching."

Callie reached under her seat, where she'd securely fastened her spare service weapon. She and Dom had developed a plan C as a backup to their backup plan, and the code word for a tag-team takedown was "chill." She just needed to point and shoot. She knew that the art of negotiation would be wasted on Simon, and waiting for Dom's cue, she was ready.

Emily, noticing that Callie was armed, looked over at her and shook her head, no. She then patted her dad's hand, as if to indicate that she knew what she was doing, and said, "Simon! Thank God you're here! I don't want to leave you. I love you."

Simon said, "It's okay, Emily. I knew you'd never leave of your own accord. Come, my angel. We're going home."

He backed Dom further into the cabin, and Emily got up. Tom tried to keep her from going, but she jerked away from him and moved toward Simon. She took Simon by the hand and said sweetly, "It's okay. You don't need the gun anymore. They can't take me against my will. I'm in charge."

Simon lowered his gun and stuck it into the back of his pants, stepping towards the door with Emily beside him. The door hadn't yet been raised, and the steps provided Emily with a very powerful and defining moment of strength. Taking back her freedom, she let go of Simon's hand and shoved him hard, causing him to lose his footing and topple down the steps, landing in a dazed heap on the concrete.

Standing there, looking at him, she said, "As I said, I'm in charge. It's your turn to understand how it feels to be locked up."

Dom and Callie ran down the stairs to check Simon for a pulse. He was still alive, and they secured him until the federal agents appeared in the hangar to take him into custody. Tom rushed to Emily's side, telling her how proud he was of her and holding her closely while they watched Simon being cuffed and taken into custody.

Callie went to check on the pilots, who were still confined in the corner of the cockpit. Tom came in to examine them, just to be sure they were okay to fly, and once they were given the thumbs up and cleared for takeoff, the jet, and a very happy and exhausted Tom, Emily, Callie and Dom, flew up and over Music City's beautiful skyline into the clouds. A debt had been repaid, and now it was time for everyone to revitalize, heal, and rest. And there was no better place to do that than the ranch.

Chapter 6: Whose Surprise is This Anyway?

Back at the Ranch...

After delivering Callie safely home to gather up her mail from the neighbor, shower, unpack, shower again, and relax, Dom brought Tom and Emily to the ranch to continue to bond. Emily still had very few memories of her dad, so Dom thought a few days' retreat at the lodge he'd built for Callie would be a tranquil place to find them again.

Dom dropped them off and gave them the keys to the truck out back, in case of emergency. Emily was about Callie's size, and Dom told her that until Callie could take her shopping in the next few days, that the closet was full of clothes she could wear during her stay with her dad.

Before Dom left, Tom took a sample of Emily's blood and asked if Dom would drop it off at a private lab he'd contacted in Austin, and he agreed. Tom thought that it was possible that Emily's memory loss was drug induced. Given Simon's psychological profile, it wouldn't be a stretch to believe he'd use drugs to control her.

About three hours later, Callie drove up to find Yin-Yang and DD standing at the fence along the front of the property. It was unusual to see them up front, but she was anxious to love on them for a few minutes. She put the car in park and got out to go over and pet them. They were excited to see her, as evidenced by their whinnying and nodding of their heads. Rubbing their faces with her hands, she said, "Where's your daddy? Did he let you out to run around and play for a while?"

After a few minutes of petting and talking to them, she drove up to the house to look for Dom. She didn't see him outside anywhere, and she called for him but got no answer. His truck was parked in front of the house, so he was bound to be somewhere nearby. She walked in the front door and called out to him, but still, no answer. He wasn't on the deck, in the bedroom, the shower. The house was empty. She thought she'd give him a call, but noticed his cell phone on the kitchen counter.

Getting a little concerned, she walked over to the stables and called out once again, but there was still no answer. It was at this point that she became very concerned. She frantically looked into each of the stalls in the stable, and on the fourth stall down, she finally found him lying in the hay. *Please, Lord, let him be okay*, she prayed silently.

She got closer to him and then saw the beautiful rise and fall of his chest. Her pulse began to slow and she whispered, "Thank you, God." He was lying there so peacefully. He must have been so exhausted that he had just laid down in the hay and closed his eyes.

Standing there watching him breathe and thinking about

how she felt just moments before, when she thought something had happened to him, led her to a decision she'd never even considered before. In all of the months they'd been together, it hadn't occurred to her just how she'd feel if he wasn't in her life. Being with Dom had changed everything in such a dramatic way. Working together as partners had only made their bond stronger, and she wanted more... more of him, more love, more commitment.

Her conservative upbringing had always gotten in the way of what she really wanted when it came to love. Wait for the man, wait for the proper time, wait, wait, wait. She was a grown woman now, a grandma, for goodness' sakes! What was she waiting for? She was an independent woman who knew what she wanted, and it was time to take action. She would surprise him at the right moment and ask him to be her husband.

The horses must have picked up on Callie's scent, because they came galloping into the stables as soon as the proposal crossed Callie's mind, and their noise woke Dom up. He sat straight up from the hay and saw Callie standing there, smiled and said, "Are we in Oz, Darlin'?"

Callie laughed and said, "Only if I get to be the good witch, Cowboy."

Getting up to his feet, he pulled her into his arms, kissed her lightly on the lips and then said, "You can be whoever you want to be, as long as I get to play a part."

They put the horses back in their stalls, made sure they were fed and watered, and walked back hand in hand to the house for a laid-back evening of welcome peace and quiet. All the noise was turned off, and they went to bed to enjoy each other without interruption.

At around 5:00 a.m., without an alarm, Callie got up and made coffee, put a sweater on and went to the deck. Dom joined her for a lovely sunrise view before heading into town to take Emily's bloodwork to the lab. Callie decided to go with him because he'd be gone for several hours, and they needed to restock groceries for the barbecue they'd decided to throw on Friday in celebration of Emily's safe return home.

After a leisurely few hours on the deck, they got dressed and drove into Austin. The bloodwork was dropped off and they were told that the report would be ready by noon, so that gave them three hours to pick up all the ingredients for a Texas-sized barbeque. After their errands were finished, they stopped by Thundercloud to chow down on the best sandwiches Austin had to offer.

Thundercloud was only a five-minute drive from the lab, so they pulled into the parking lot of the lab with about 10 minutes to spare. They were chatting about their crazy trip to France and Tennessee when Dom's phone rang. Callie could only hear Dom's end of the call, but it went something like...

"Yeah, man. Fantastic. How are you? Oh, really? Wow! I know I'd love it, but let me check with my lady. Hang on a sec."

Muting the phone, Dom said, "Hey, Dane, one of my neighbors, is calling to ask if we might like to take a balloon ride tomorrow morning around 7:00. Are you game?"

Callie thought for a second and said, "Hmm... let me check my schedule. Oh, wait. I have no job, so sure!"

They both laughed, and Dom was still laughing as he unmuted the phone to tell Dane they'd love to and thank him for the invitation. Callie told Dom that she'd never been in a hot air balloon, but the festivals were such a beautiful sight to see, and she'd always wanted to jump into one. To Callie's amazement, Dom had never had the experience either, which made them both that much more excited about it. It was something that they could experience together for the first time.

When the phone call ended, Dom walked into the lab and the lab tech handed him the envelope. He walked back out, got in the truck, and they went back to the ranch to deliver the report to Tom. Emily was sitting on the front porch of the lodge when they pulled up, and Callie commented to Dom how beautiful and serene she looked sitting in the swing.

Tom walked out onto the front porch as they were getting out of the truck, and Dom handed him the report. Perusing the report, he realized that his thoughts about the drugs had been confirmed. The lab findings were positive for benzodiazepines, more specifically Rohypnol. Dom and Callie were both familiar with it in the criminal setting, because it was prevalent in rape cases. You could spike anyone's drink with it, and it could affect both short-term and long-term memory. Dom surmised that Simon was probably drugging the tea that she drank every morning, keeping her constantly fuzzy.

Tom had been giving her plenty of water over the past 24 hours, but he was going to have to prescribe a smaller dosage of it in order to wean her off of it. It was a very addictive drug, and he wanted to be sure she got the proper medical care. Of course, counseling was also going to have to be a part of Emily's recovery. She had already spoken with Tom about that, but she needed some time to regroup before she committed to the work that was going to be necessary to reclaim her mental health.

Dom placed a call to his personal physician, explained the situation, and put Tom on the phone with him so that they could get started on the process of getting the prescription. Dom's doctor agreed to meet them at the community clinic down the road from the ranch to make it easier for her. Dom invited the two of them for the Friday barbecue, and he and Callie went back up to the house while Tom and Emily got directions and went to the clinic for her meds.

Once the groceries were put away, Dom and Callie decided to take a horseback ride down the trail to the eastern edge of the property. He was looking at developing that for the main bed and breakfast for the dude ranch, but he wanted Callie's opinion about it before he reached out to investors. A road would have to be built, but everything had already been cleared for that.

It was a gorgeous spring day with a cool breeze but plenty of sunshine, and the ride only took 30 minutes or so. Dom explained that he chose this piece of the ranch for the bed and breakfast because it was the most picturesque view of the Pedernales River and the rolling hills that blocked the city's skyline, which allowed the stars to shine brightly all on their own. He thought it would give visitors the ranch experience with the convenience of being close to the city.

Once Callie saw the property, she was in total agreement and could envision it exactly the way he described it. She just couldn't soak up enough of Dom. He was a man of many talents, and she was thrilled to be discovering them all.

Walking the property and watering the horses had taken longer than they'd thought it would, and the sun was beginning to go down by the time they finished. They'd need to leave right away to be sure to get back to the house while there was still light for the path, so they saddled up and started back.

It was nearly dark when Dom and Callie got back to the

stables with the horses and put them down for the night. They were starving, but neither of them felt like cooking or cleaning, and because they needed an early start for their balloon adventure the following morning, they got in the truck and went to the Burger Barn to treat themselves to the specialty of the house. It was called the Texas Breakfast, which essentially was a burger topped with strips of bacon, a fried egg and a slice of melted cheddar cheese. They shared an order of fries to relieve at least some of the guilt and the caloric indulgence.

They left the Burger Barn equally satisfied, lethargic, and extremely grateful that it was a short drive home. Callie dropped her purse on the kitchen counter. Dom kicked off his boots in the same spot and followed her into the bedroom, where they both fell onto the bed. They set the alarm for 5:30 a.m., and after a single kiss goodnight, without taking the time to undress, they were goners.

The beeping of Dom's cell phone alarm went off as scheduled, and he got up to get coffee and a light breakfast ready while Callie showered and got ready. When she came walking into the kitchen wearing her red boots, jeans, and the lacy white pullover she'd bought the day before, he told her how beautiful she looked and gave her a kiss on the cheek. She sat down at the bar and ate her bagel and coffee, and Dom went to take his turn in the shower.

In 15 minutes, he was back and ready to get out the door, so they drove over to Dane's ranch, where they found Dane and his glorious hot air balloon. It was every color in the rainbow, with a gold Texas star right in the middle. Dom introduced the two, and Dane went about giving Dom practice lessons on how to work the mechanics of the balloon. In just a few attempts, Dom looked like a real pro, and they were ready to hop in and lift off and float over the countryside.

Rising to an altitude just above the treetops, Dom let the balloon float for a while. Callie was struck by the moment. The opportunity couldn't be more perfect. They were completely alone, floating along without distraction through the sky. So without hesitation, she began her unprepared, unrehearsed proposal.

"Hey, Babe..."

"Yes?"

"... I was just thinking about how many adventures we've been through together over the last five months. It's pretty remarkable if you think about it, isn't it?"

"That's an understatement, Darlin'. We've survived a murder, a near drowning, the barrel of a gun, and several criminals, in more than one country."

"Wow! It sounds like a movie, when you bullet point it all out that way. You know, my daddy used to say that you know you're with the right person if you can't imagine your life without them."

"Wise man, that daddy of yours."

"I always thought so too. Before we met, I thought I had everything I needed, but you've shown me things that I never knew existed. When I found you asleep in the barn the other day, I have to admit that I lost it a little. I thought something had happened to you."

Dom put his arm around her and said, "I'm sorry, Darlin'. Why didn't you say something?"

Callie paused for a minute, searching for the right words, and then said, "Because I was waiting for the right words to tell you that I've found a home with you, and I never want to leave. I love you, and I never really knew what that meant until now. Whatever life we have left on this earth, I want to wake up lying next to you every morning. Will you marry me, Cowboy?"

And there they were. The words came tumbling out, and the look on Dom's face was inexplicable. He appeared to be spooked, but Callie couldn't tell because he was speechless. She gave him a second to take it in, and just as she was about to throw herself out of the balloon to escape humiliation and rejection, Dom raised his eyebrows and said, "Are you kidding me right now?"

Callie was dumbfounded. She knew he'd be a little

shocked by her forwardness, but she didn't expect him to insult her. Stuck in a loop of confusion, she finally said, "No, I'm not kidding you. What kind of response is that?"

Dom took his hands, put them softly on her face and said, "Look down, Darlin'."

Still confused about why he wouldn't answer her question and what could be more important down below, she looked over the edge of the balloon as they were floating over an enormous field of bluebonnets and she saw that that they spelled out the words, "Will you marry me, Callie?"

Callie began to laugh, and so did Dom, as they counted from one, two, three, and yelled a simultaneous "Yes," and kissed. Callie said, "I'm so sorry, Babe. I totally ruined your surprise with my surprise."

Dom pulled her close and whispered in her ear, "On the contrary. You upstaged my proposal, which turned out to be a win-win. Who could argue those odds? So I guess this means you're buying the rings, right?"

Callie laughed and said, "Good one, Cowboy. I don't need a ring. I have a cowboy and a horse."

Dom just smiled and began to take the balloon down. Callie wasn't sure what he was doing until she looked ahead into the distance and saw a gazebo in the middle of the empty field. The balloon descended further, and Dom dumped the weights out onto the ground beneath, hopped out and lifted Callie out, securing the balloon in place shortly after.

Now steady on her feet, Callie noticed that the grassy path leading to the gazebo was covered with red rose petals. They walked hand in hand across the petals, and Dom said, "Did you say something about our lives being a movie? I've laid a red carpet for my leading lady."

Callie was so excited that she could barely breathe. They made their way to the gazebo and underneath was a small table covered in a white linen tablecloth, a bucket of iced French champagne, and lying next to it was a ring box. Dom poured the champagne and they toasted to their future together.

Giving Callie a wink, he picked up the ring box and said, "I guess you don't even need to see what's in the box since you're good with the cowboy and the horse."

Callie grabbed his hand and said, "Probably not, but it wouldn't hurt to take a tiny peek, since you went through all this trouble."

Opening up the ring box for her, Dom took out the most exquisite 4-carat princess-cut ruby Callie had ever seen. It was surrounded by tiny diamonds and set in platinum. He placed it on her finger, it fit perfectly, and she decided she was never taking it off... because it matched her cowgirl boots.

For the next hour, they sat under the gazebo and finished

the bottle of champagne while they talked about their dreams for their future. Dom wanted Callie to help him get the dude ranch off the ground, and given Callie's recent decision to retire from the courtroom and move to freelance, she jumped at the opportunity to be involved in such a wonderful project. They wanted to settle into a comfortable, slower pace and take the time to nourish each other and spend more time with family.

It was for that reason that they decided to get married quickly and quietly, perhaps with just a simple daytrip to Las Vegas. There was really no reason to go big with a wedding at this point in their lives. They'd already done that with their first marriages, and they placed no real value in making a big fussy event with tons of drama.

They got back into the balloon and were excited to get back home and start calling their family and friends to share their very happy news. The balloon ride back somehow looked prettier to Callie. Her heart was full, and looking up into the heavens, she closed her eyes for a moment and thanked God for blessing her with a love that she knew would be her last. She gently kissed Dom on the neck and smiled up at him with pride. *He's mine. He's all mine*, she thought.

Dane was waiting in the pasture below when they landed, and was grinning from ear to ear when he helped Callie out of the balloon. Evidently, he'd been in on Dom's surprise, and was waiting for them to share the result. Callie showed him her ring, and Dom shook his hand, thanking him for all of his help, and then returned to the ranch to begin making phone calls to family and friends.

Everyone they spoke to was excited to hear the news. After the phone calls, they went to deliver the news in person to Dom's mother. She told them she was very happy for them, and when Dom got up to get her a glass of water, she took the opportunity to tell Callie that she'd never seen her son so happy, and that she was very excited to be getting a new daughter. Callie told her that she loved her and that she was thrilled to be a part of her family.

The excitement of the day was beginning to take a toll on both Callie and Dom, so they hugged and kissed his mom and made their way back to Callie's house to take a nap. They'd go back to the ranch in the morning, but they would settle in at Callie's for the night.

Day turned into evening, and they began to check on flights to Las Vegas for the following week. They could get to Vegas in the morning, get their license 15 minutes later, be married within the hour and back in Austin before dinner if they timed it right. They'd sleep on it and make the reservations after talking to Tom and Emily at the barbecue, because they didn't want them to feel rushed into going back home.

Going upstairs to bed after a light dinner of potato soup,

Dom opened up the covers for Callie to get in. Nestling her body up as close to him as she could, he wrapped his arms around her and watched as she admired her ring. He said, "I have never fallen in love before. I have loved, but I've never fallen. To steal a line from Barry White, *you're the first, my last, my everything.*"

Callie said in a soft voice, "Aww... I think they should play that when we walk down the aisle in Vegas. Do you think they would substitute Barry for Elvis?"

Dom laughed and said, "For an extra dollar, and they'd probably throw in the breakfast buffet and a few tokens for the slot machines."

Callie chuckled and said, "I'll bet you're right."

They stayed up telling cheesy Vegas jokes for the next hour or so, and then purposely decided to forgo setting a morning alarm. There was nothing on the agenda for the following day anyway, except the barbeque with Tom and Emily. Callie couldn't wait to share their happy news with them, which kept her up a little later than Dom, but after wrapping herself up in his warm body, she drifted off to sleep.

Alarm notwithstanding, Callie woke up at her usual 5:00 a.m., but decided to stay in bed next to her cowboy until he opened his eyes. She wanted to be the first thing to show up when he flashed his gorgeous blue eyes, which turned out to be only five minutes later. Apparently, neither of them could evade their internal body clocks, and so they snuggled and kissed good morning for a few more minutes before they got up and went downstairs to make breakfast as a newly engaged couple.

The happiness in the room was clear as Dom began to whistle. Callie hadn't heard him do that before, and she made the comment that it reminded her of the old black-and-white western movies that her dad used to watch. She'd seen them all at least a hundred times over the course of her life. Every time he'd visit her in Austin, he'd turn on the Cowboy Channel, and they'd watch all of them over again even though he had the lines memorized.

"Yeah, my dad loved the old westerns too," Dom said. "The way the older cowboys were depicted in film made my dad proud of his lifestyle. We were raised on them, but we also lived by their principles. I walked away from the lifestyle in my youth, thinking that I wanted something fancier, more exciting, but what I've found is that there's nothing more exciting than being your authentic self. This is who I was meant to be, and I wouldn't trade it for anything in the world."

Callie listened as he spoke and realized how fortunate each of them were to have found happiness, both inside of themselves and with each other. It was the perfect union. What Dom verbalized was so profound, but he probably didn't even realize it because he was a cowboy in the truest sense of the word.

"I love that you found your way back to the ranch, because

it ultimately led to finding your way to me," Callie responded.

"I couldn't have said that better, Darlin'. Our lives are about to become sweeter than we ever imagined."

"I am so excited that I can barely breathe!" Callie said, twirling around in the kitchen. "We're getting married, Babe!"

Dom's eyes widened, as did his smile, and he asked, "How about a little celebration music?"

"Perfect!" Callie replied.

Dom pulled up one of his favorite radio streaming apps and turned it to the country love songs channel, and then he walked over and held his hand out for Callie. She took his hand and they began to two-step around the kitchen and out onto the patio. When the song was over, he gently dipped her and then pulled her back close to his lips, kissing her softly.

They then went back into the kitchen to eat a nice breakfast, and the rest of the day was spent lounging around at the ranch. Dom called Tom around 2:00, letting him know that they were welcome to join him and Callie whenever they felt like coming up; that they were just going to be hanging out poolside before dinner. Tom said that sounded great and they'd probably be up around 6:00.

With the steaks marinating and all the meal prep done by 4:00, Dom and Callie brewed a pot of coffee and set out various bottles of wine, soft drinks and a special bottle of champagne for later and stepped out to the patio. Tom and Emily rang the bell just before 6:00 and Dom showed them out to the pool area.

Callie greeted them with a smile and said, "Hey, Emily, do you think you'd be up for a little shopping tomorrow? I know a cool little shop near my house where we could find some beautiful things for you to wear. I'm sure you're probably tired of wearing borrowed things."

Emily replied, "If it wouldn't be too much trouble, I'd really enjoy getting out for a little while and spending some time with you."

"Then we'll make a morning of it. We can take in a little shopping and lunch at my favorite tapas restaurant, with a beautiful view of the lake," Callie said.

"That sounds amazing!" Emily responded.

Emily looked rested and Tom appeared happier than Dom and Callie had seen him before. Emily shared that a few of her memories had begun to come back over the past few days, with the slow flushing of drugs out of her system. She was still relatively quiet, but Callie knew that was to be expected, given the circumstances.

Callie got up to get coffee for everyone, and when she served Tom his cup, he noticed the extra red sparkle on her finger. He said, "So does anyone have anything they'd like to share?"

Dom smiled and said, "Boy, you don't miss a trick, do

you?"

Tom said, "It's kind of hard to miss a bright red rock like that, Dom."

Callie blushed slightly, and Emily insisted on seeing it at that point. Then Dom shared the story of the simultaneous proposals from the day before. Dom's recounting of their balloon ride brought laughter from Tom and Emily, as well as hugs and congratulations. When Callie mentioned that they were going to have a quickie Vegas wedding, Tom and Emily agreed with everyone else they'd told, saying that a love as great as theirs deserved a grand celebration. But Callie insisted that the real celebration was the marriage, and that they didn't want to make a big event out of the wedding.

At around 7:15, Dom and Callie's Texas feast was served. When dinner was finished, the champagne was poured, with sparkling cider for Emily. Glasses were lifted for a happy future for Tom and Emily, and then for Dom and Callie. Emily began to get tired, so Tom took her back to the lodge shortly after 10:00. Callie would pick Emily up at about 9:00 the following morning.

It was getting cooler outside, so Dom got up and lit a fire outside and he and Callie sat down nearby to finish off the rest of the champagne and discuss in more detail their trip to Vegas. They didn't mention to Tom and Emily a specific date, because it just didn't seem like the right time. They'd only been at the ranch for a few days, and Dom felt like they needed more time to decompress before going home.

Callie agreed with him, and so they decided maybe they'd wait a few weeks until everything settled down. Vegas wasn't going anywhere, and there was no real need to rush, even though they were anxious to become husband and wife as soon as possible.

With that decision made and the champagne bottle empty, they went inside to clean the kitchen and then went to bed. It had been a fantastic 24 hours, and they were grateful for the time off, but Dom had to mend a few fences around the property, and he wanted to get a jump on that as soon as the sun rose because it would take a better part of the day to finish.

The champagne had helped counter the excitement and the endorphins, and sleep came very quickly for Callie. Dom must have been extremely tired, because Callie didn't feel him move from the spot next to her the entire night.

When the alarm went off at 7:00, Callie reached over for Dom and then realized that he was already up and out of the house. She groggily turned over in the bed, and next to her on Dom's pillow was a note, with a single bluebonnet lying on top. She picked up the note and could smell his cologne on it, and then when her eyes came into focus, she read the note.

My love, my life, my soon-to-be wife, you are the

bluebonnets in the spring, the snowfall in the winter, the flowing waterfall in the summer, and the golden leaves in the autumn. For every season, you are the reason my heart smiles. Your soon-to-be husband.

Callie brought the piece of paper to her lips, and her eyes filled with tears. *Where did this man come from?* He was truly a gift that continued to give, as evidenced by the fact that in addition to this beautiful note he'd written, she could smell the fresh pot of coffee he'd started for her before he left.

She got up, had a cup of coffee, got showered and changed, and left the house around 8:45. Emily was waiting for her on the front porch when she got there. Tom stepped out front to say hello and give Emily money, and the two women headed off to shop.

Emily and Callie had a wonderful day of shopping and lunch, and it allowed Emily to open up a little and talk about her time with Simon. She had only recently learned the truth about Simon from her dad, and it was quite painful to realize that she'd been kidnapped and sold to the highest bidder, as if she weren't a human being. But she was grateful that she was alive, that she hadn't been physically hurt by him, and that she was finally free of him.

Callie told her that she'd done a little checking on whether Simon was actually married to Emily, and that thankfully, the marriage was also a lie. She wouldn't have to testify because Simon had agreed to plead guilty to lessen his sentence, and she also wouldn't have to go through any civil proceeding to secure a divorce. Emily was grateful to hear all of that, because it allowed her to move to the next phase of her life without being stuck in the legal system.

After sharing that information with Emily, Callie quickly changed the subject to a happier, more positive one, and began to talk about her future with Dom and the plans for the bed and breakfast. She then asked about Emily's thoughts about what she might like to do with her life when she returned home.

Emily said that she'd always loved music; that she'd sung in her church choir and could play the guitar, so she thought she might pursue a career in music. Callie told her that she thought that was a wonderful career choice and offered her assistance in the event she ever needed it. Callie knew a few people in the music industry in Austin, and she told Emily she'd be happy to make a few phone calls to get more information for her about where to begin in that pursuit.

Emily smiled and thanked Callie for her offer, telling her that she'd be sure to let her know once everything settled down with her life. It appeared to be a good day for Emily, and Callie was thrilled that she could be a part of bringing a smile to this young woman's face, at least for a day. She'd been through such a horrific experience, but hopefully she would be able to overcome it in a relatively short time.

Callie dropped Emily off at the lodge around 1:30 and drove back to the ranch to see if Dom had finished working on the fences. He hadn't made it back yet, so she decided to go back to her house to relax and do nothing for the rest of the afternoon.

On her way back home, she got a call from Ali. He rarely called in the middle of the day, because the kids kept him hopping, especially on the weekend. She answered the phone quickly, and Ali said, "Hey, Mom. What's up?"

Callie responded, "Hey, Baby! Just headed home from the ranch for a bit. What's up with you?"

"Two things: I have a job interview in Austin next Friday, and I was going to bring Cass and the kids for the weekend, if it's okay."

"Of course! It's more than okay! I'm excited anytime I get to see you guys. What's the second thing?"

"Sophia and Michael want to know if you and Dom will take them to the zoo on Saturday. Is that possible?"

"You tell them they can count on me. I'll have to check with Dom, but I'm sure he'd love it if he doesn't have anything going on."

"Can you check with him and let me know before I tell them? They specifically asked for him."

Callie smiled and said, "You bet, Baby. I'll give him a call and call you in a while."

"Great! Well, I've got to let you go. We're about to put the kids down for a nap. Love you!"

"Love you too, Baby! Kisses and hugs to everyone. I'll text you when I talk to Dom about the zoo. See you soon!"

Callie hung up the phone just as she was pulling into her driveway. Once she got situated and relaxed inside, she picked up the phone to call Dom. He was mending the final fence, but told her that he'd be over later and would bring dinner. When she asked about the trip to the zoo with the kids, he said that he wouldn't think of missing that. He was excited to spend time with them.

They ended the call, and Callie changed into her pajamas and sat down on the couch to veg out in front of the television. It didn't take long for her to fall asleep, only to be awakened by a knock on the door from Dom three hours later. She greeted him in her pajamas, which was unusual for her in the middle of the day, but he commented on how beautiful she looked. She rolled her eyes and said, "You really do want to marry me, don't you?"

Dom smiled and said, "Darlin', there's not a man in the world who would say no to you. I'm just lucky enough to have snapped you up before they got to you."

Callie responded, "I'm the lucky one, Cowboy," kissing him

on the lips and grabbing the food from him to take it into the kitchen.

They ate a grilled chicken salad for dinner, leaving room for the two slices of strawberry cheesecake Dom had gotten for dessert, and then afterwards began to talk about the details of the wedding, what Callie's plans were for her house, and the business end of the ranch going forward. There were a lot of details that needed to be worked out, but Callie's house was paid for, so there was no need to put it on the market. She'd planned to leave it to the kids, and so she'd talk to them about it soon.

The weekend flew by, as well as the following week. After Dom and Callie's discussion about the bed and breakfast for the dude ranch, he'd reached out to his investors and they'd given the go-ahead on the road construction, so Dom had been busy managing that. Callie had spent the week visiting with Emily and Tom and preparing for her visit with Ali, Cass and the kids.

Friday finally came, and Lauren called around 9:00, saying that she was coming to town as well. The house was filling up pretty quickly, so Callie quickly ran to the market to be sure she had enough to feed everyone for the weekend.

When she returned from the grocery store, Ali called to say they were just around the corner, asking if she needed anything. She told him she'd just picked up everything, and that his sister would be joining them later for dinner. Ali dropped Cass and the kids off, quickly said hello to Callie, and then went off to his job interview. Callie hadn't even had a chance to ask him what that was all about, but Cass filled her in with the details while Ali was gone. If it worked out, they'd be moving back to Austin. It was a great opportunity for Ali, and the kids weren't in school yet, so it would be an easy transition for them.

Callie couldn't help but hope that it did work out, because number one, she'd love to have them closer so that she could see more of Sophia and Michael; and two, the timing was perfect because they could just move right into her house when she moved to the ranch.

Cass fed the kids soup and a sandwich, and Callie put them down for a nap. About an hour later, Ali called Cass to tell her that he'd been hired on the spot. When she hung up, she was a little dazed from the news, but excited nonetheless; even more so when Callie explained that they could put their house on the market and move right away.

Ali drove up just as the kids were getting up from their nap, and Lauren walked in the door about an hour after that. Callie was thrilled to have the noise of children in the house again. Life for her family was about to change in a huge way. She'd be leaving the house they grew up in, but there was something so wonderful about handing the keys over to the next generation and walking into her new life with Dom.

As Cass started getting an early dinner prepared, Ali, Lauren and Callie went out to the patio to sit down and talk about their wishes with respect to the house. Callie told them that she and Dom had delayed their trip to Vegas for a few weeks because of Tom and Emily, but she could move at any time. Ali and Lauren agreed that it would work out perfectly if Ali, Cass and the kids could just move in whenever they were ready. Lauren was traveling a lot anyway, and she had no need for ties at the moment, but Ali told her that she could stay there whenever she wanted to; that it would always be her home too.

With the details of the house settled, they went inside to help with dinner and play with the kids. Dom arrived about 30 minutes later, and when he walked into the house, Michael and Sophia ran up for a hug. After he said hello to everyone, he sat down on the couch by Callie, and Sophia hopped up into his lap.

He was in midsentence with Callie when Sophia tapped him on the face. He looked at her, smiling, and said, "Yes, ma'am?"

She said, "Can I call you Papa now?"

He looked at her and said, "Baby girl, I can't think of a nicer name than that. I'd be proud to be your papa."

Sophia then leaned over and gave him a kiss on the cheek. And as Callie looked across the room, everyone in the room was smiling. It was clear that he was now a part of Callie's family.

Sophia had just placed her stamp of approval on him.

She got up from his lap, walked over to her little brother, pointed at Dom and said, "Michael, this is Papa. Can you say Papa?"

Michael looked up from the truck he was playing with and said, "Yes. Papa."

Dom was basking in the glow of his new family. Callie could see it in his eyes. He was going to be an amazing grandfather. He could now teach the next generation about the cowboy lifestyle and everything that went along with that.

Michael and Sophia went back to arguing over toys, and Callie got up to help Cass with dinner while Dom and Ali got to know each other better. They stepped out to the patio for a few minutes, and Callie had no idea what they were talking about, but knowing both of them the way she did, she knew it had something to do with their love for her. She saw them shake hands, then hug, and it seemed as if her son had given his approval, which was incredibly important to her.

After dinner, Dom and Callie gave the kids a bath while Ali, Cass and Lauren started a game of Clue. Sophia insisted that Dom tell her a bedtime story, so Callie went in to put Michael down. Afterwards, they both went back downstairs to sit in on a round, and when that was over, it was time for bed. They said their goodnights and everyone went to their respective rooms.

The following morning, Michael was the first up at 6:30. Sophia got up five minutes later, and Callie took them downstairs for breakfast and cartoons. An hour later, everyone else was up and at the table for pancakes, bacon and eggs and coffee. The zoo opened at 8:30, and the kids were getting anxious, so Ali got them ready while Dom and Callie went out to swap out the car seats.

Plans had previously been made for Dom and Callie to bring the kids to the ranch after the zoo, and then the rest of the family would join them at the ranch for dinner. Once the kids were buckled in, Dom and Callie set out for their zoo adventure.

What started out as a trip to the zoo turned into three hours there, lunch and games at Chuck E. Cheese's and a trip to the toy store, because Dom insisted on ending the day with gifts. Seven hours later, they pulled up to the front gates of the ranch.

The gates opened and they drove a few hundred feet, and Dom stopped. Cars were parked everywhere, and Dom leaned over to Callie and said, "Darlin', just how many people did we invite to this family get-together?

Callie, equally shocked, said, "What the heck is going on?"

They pulled in to park in Dom's usual place, got the kids out, and walked in the front door. And as they did, a room full of their family and friends yelled, "Surprise!"

This scared Michael, and he ran over to his dad, who was standing in front of the crowd of smiling people. Dom and Callie were still standing there, totally confused about what they'd just walked into.

Ali became the spokesperson of the group and said, "Welcome to Tex-Vegas. Did you really think you could get away with leaving us out of your wedding? We all got together because we wanted to show you how much you both mean to us. You've spent a lifetime taking care of all of your friends and your family. We wanted you to have the kind of wedding that celebrates not only the amazing love you've found in each other, but also the amazing people that you are.

"We've left out no details. All you have to do is shower and change. You met over a sunset, and the people you see in this room have worked hard to ensure that you begin your life as husband and wife in the same way."

Dom and Callie were speechless and in tears. Lauren walked up to her mom, hugged her and took her by the hand.

"Let's go, Mom. Your bridal party is waiting upstairs."

Dom's son, Christopher, stepped out from behind Ali, and Dom began to quiver a little. Dom had no idea he was even in town. They had really pulled off a Texas-sized coup.

Christopher walked up, gave his dad a hug, and said, "Dad, your groomsmen are waiting to help you get ready as well. Let's get this party started."

Dom and Callie looked at each other and shrugged their

shoulders. They weren't about to get in the way of all of this love. So off they went to get showered and changed.

Two hours later, Callie was ready. She had been greeted upstairs by Pam, who told her that Lauren and Ali had orchestrated the entire event, with the help of Christopher, Dom's mother, Pam, Tom and Emily, and numerous other friends and neighbors whose lives they'd touched along the way.

Lauren had a friend in Dallas design Callie's dress and deliver it to Pam. Pam unzipped the bag it was in to reveal the most stunning gown Callie had ever laid her eyes on. It was a strapless silk gown, with hand-beaded pearls along the top of the curved bodice in the front, and a flowing calf-length skirt, allowing the perfect view of her red cowgirl boots, which Lauren brought from Callie's closet. Cass had made her headdress, which was a beautiful but simple ribbon-covered band with pearls and rhinestones set in place.

Callie looked at Lauren, tearing up again, and said, "I have never been prouder of you than I am today. Thank you, my love. What an amazing gift you are. I love you."

Lauren smiled and replied, "I love you too, Mom. Now, stop crying and get dressed. Your chariot awaits."

Pam dabbed Callie's eyes with a tissue and helped her finish getting dressed and downstairs. Approaching the top of the stairs, she saw Dom standing there, looking better than a cowboy had a right to, in his black tuxedo and red cummerbund and bowtie. She got to the bottom of the stairs, and he took her hand, saying, "Darlin', I can't believe I get to call you mine. Let's hurry before the spell breaks."

Callie laughed and walked with him to the front door, and Dane, shaking his hand, opened the door to reveal a carriage that looked like something out of a Disney movie. It was hitched to both Yin-Yang and DD, and Tom was standing beside it in his tuxedo.

He helped Dom and Callie into the carriage, got up into the seat and set the horses in motion for parts unknown. Within five minutes, they pulled up to a beautiful area of the ranch that had been transformed into a wedding venue like none other. Right before them, in the middle of the pasture, a deck had been built in the shape of Texas. Half was painted black, the other half white, and there was a great big red heart painted in the middle. Guests were already seated in linen-covered chairs on both sides of an aisle that had been covered with a red runway carpet. It was truly a vision of beauty.

Callie and Dom sat in the carriage for a few minutes, taking in the magic that lay before their eyes. All of the hard work and love that had gone into creating this spectacular event for them was overwhelming.

In just a few short minutes, as if it had been rehearsed

many times, the groomsmen and bridesmaids were standing on either side of the carriage, and the music began to play as Ali reached up for Callie's hand to help her out of the carriage. Dom got out on the other side and walked up to stand and wait for her on one side of the heart on the deck, with Tom and Christopher joining him.

Sophia and Michael, who had been standing with Cass, had apparently been designated ring bearer and flower girl. They made their way down the aisle, followed by the bridesmaids, and then, to Callie's surprise, Emily took the stage and sang a beautiful rendition of, *Cowboy Take Me Away*, as Ali put her hand under his elbow and said, "Let's do this, Mom."

He walked her up to Dom, kissed her on the cheek, and placed her hand in Dom's before joining the other groomsmen. At that point, Dom's minister, Reverend Milner, took the stage and began the ceremony. Since Dom and Callie hadn't known about the ceremony, they hadn't had time to prepare any vows, but there were no words that hadn't already been said between them. So in lieu of that, the minister read one of his favorite poems by Kahlil Gibran, which turned out to be Callie's favorite. He followed that with Dom's favorite, 1 Corinthians, Chapter 13.

They were announced husband and wife after exchanging the rings and their promises to love and cherish each other, and as impossible as it seemed, the timing couldn't have been more perfect. Dom kissed Callie just as the sun set over the Austin skyline.

Dom and Callie had just experienced a fairytale wedding, and even though they weren't legally married at this point, they knew their union was blessed by God, their family, and their friends. The legal stuff was just a piece of paper, and it could easily be remedied in the coldness of some clerk's office while they were running other errands. For now, it had no meaning at all to them.

Dom and Callie took the carriage back to the house, where food had been catered by the Burger Barn, the champagne was flowing freely, and the cake was chocolate... because who needs vanilla? It was a fun-filled reception, full of music and laughter and love.

After the guests left, the kids retreated to their rooms at the ranch, and Dom and Callie celebrated privately on the deck. Dom took Callie into his arms and said, "Well, hasn't this been a week full of surprises. I planned a surprise proposal, and you planned one that threw mine for a loop. And now this? I guess they showed us a thing or two about surprises, didn't they?"

"Here's to a lifetime full of wonderful surprises, Cowboy. As a matter of fact, I think I can almost guarantee another one is about to come your way," Callie said, taking him by the hand and leading him to the bedroom.

A few short days later, the kids were gone, and Callie was at her house packing up her clothes to take back to the ranch. She would make the final move at some point, but for now, she just wanted to get her clothes and a few other necessities so that she didn't have to keep going back and forth for them. But until Ali moved the family in, there was no rush to move the larger things. She hadn't realized how many clothes she had in her closet until she tried to pack it all in a few suitcases, but she had a few boxes that she was able to use to finish up the job.

With the car packed up, she drove back to the ranch to pick Dom up for a late lunch. Driving around the last curve before reaching the gate, she saw a banner hanging over the ranch sign, so she stopped to look up when she got close enough to read it. The sign said, "Welcome home, Darlin'." She'd never felt more welcome, more at home, than she felt on this ranch with her cowboy.